What could happen?

"Hey, look at that hitchhiker," Christina interrupted. She slowed the car.

"Oh, no!" Terri declared firmly. "No way. No way, Christina."

"But look how cute he is," Christina said, braking hard.

"Cute? He looks like a killer."

"Don't exaggerate, *mom*," Christina said, sticking her tongue out at her friend. She pulled the car to the shoulder of the highway.

The hitchhiker shifted the canvas bag he was carrying and came trotting up to Terri's side of the car. He had short blond hair, Terri saw, and startling green eyes. And he was big, muscular, like a jock, and very broad-shouldered.

"Christina — I don't like this," Terri said unhappily.

Christina laughed at her. "What could happen?"

**Other Point thrillers
by R.L. Stine:**

THE HITCHHIKER

R.L. STINE

SCHOLASTIC INC.
New York Toronto London Auckland Sydney

ISBN 0-590-46100-1

12 11 10 9 8 7 6 5 4   3 4 5 6 7 8/9

Printed in the U.S.A.   01

First Scholastic printing, January 1993

THE
HiTCHHiKER

Chapter 1

"Please don't, James. Please — don't hurt me."

He heard her voice again as he stepped onto the highway. Pleading with him. Begging him.

He heard her crying again, the loud sobs that made her shoulders tremble.

"Please don't, James."

Her anguished cries followed James as he made his escape.

If only I could control my temper, he thought.

He raised his green eyes to the tilted highway sign jutting up from the sandy highway shoulder. Highway 1.

The sun had set a few hours before as he made his way out of Key West. Now, even though it was dark, the air remained daylight hot, heavy, and wet. Swampy.

"Got to get away," he said aloud, scratching the back of his neck.

James was powerfully built for seventeen, muscular, with big shoulders and a broad, football player neck. He had short blond hair, buzzed close on the sides, a handsome face, serious, seldom smiling, and olive-green eyes that always seemed to be angry.

Angry.

Always angry.

"Please don't hurt me, James."

He heard her frightened voice again as his eyes searched the narrow highway. Shifting the small canvas bag that held his few belongings, he began walking north along the shoulder, his sneakers sinking into the sand.

"Got to get away. Got to get away."

Got to get away from her voice, her cries.

But how?

He swatted a mosquito on his forehead.

Twin white lights, creeping silently along the road as if sneaking up behind him, signaled an approaching car. James turned toward the lights and raised the thumb of his free hand.

The lights grew brighter, brighter, accompanied by a roar that broke the night silence.

He closed his eyes as the car sped past without slowing.

He waited for the lights in his head to fade.

"Please don't hurt me, James."

He began walking again, picking up his pace, kicking at the damp sand as he walked.

Maybe I'll leave Florida and never come back, he thought.

Is it possible to do that? Just walk away from your home? Leave all the bad stuff behind and never return?

Key West had always meant trouble for him. He had moved there with his aunt when he was twelve. After the accident. After both of his parents had been smeared across the highway.

What a place to grow up.

The bottom of the country.

As low as you can go.

His aunt actually liked it. She liked the crumbling old houses. The choppy, blue gulf waters. Liked the cats walking everywhere. She even liked seeing all the tourists, walking the narrow streets, looking for Hemingway's old house, lining up for the boats to take them out to the treasure-hunting reef.

James had hated Key West from the start.

Maybe it was because his parents had to die for him to get there.

Maybe it was because his aunt was so eager for him to like it.

Maybe it was just because he hated it.

He was always in trouble there. Always angry.

At first he had thought that *all* teenagers were supposed to be angry. But all of the others seemed so laid-back compared to him, so uncaring, so . . . happy.

They were only interested in their tans, in their boogie boards and snorkel equipment. In partying and looking good.

It all made James angry. All of it.

He kicked a clump of dirt onto the highway. "I'm never going back to Key West," he muttered, slapping at another mosquito.

Another car roared past.

James kept his thumb raised. A van filled with teenagers pulled up and slowed nearly to a stop. He could see grinning faces peering through the windows at him. One of the passengers waved to him. James started to jog toward the van — and it sped away, its horn honking loudly.

James raised his fist angrily.

Stupid clowns, he thought.

He wanted to kill them. *Kill* them!

"James, please don't. Please don't hurt me."

He shook his head hard as if trying to shake away her pleading voice. Once again he heard her crying, saw her shoulders tremble.

I know I should control my temper, he thought. But sometimes things get to be too much. Sometimes they just build up inside me, and build up and build up and build up — until I explode.

What can I do?

It wasn't the first time he had hurt her.

But it would be the last.

Kicking sand off his hightops, he stepped onto the highway without slowing his pace. Again he shifted the canvas bag to his other hand.

Someone's got to stop and give me a ride, he thought. I can't walk all the way North.

He walked over a narrow bridge. Water trickled softly below, the only sound except for the scuffing of his sneakers on the asphalt.

He turned and raised his thumb as lights crept up the highway. Another car. It rolled past him.

He lowered his thumb, disappointed, feeling the anger start to boil inside him.

But then the car squealed to a stop, its tires skidding onto the sandy shoulder. The red taillights glared at him like two eyes.

James jogged quickly toward the car, a black Buick Skylark.

The driver's window slid down with an electric buzz. He was an old man, James saw. With a knobby, bald head. Light glinted off his thick, round eyeglasses.

"How far you going?" the old man asked, smiling up at James, his eyes studying James's face from behind the thick glasses.

James shrugged. "I really don't know," he replied. "Just heading north."

"I'm only going as far as Fort Lauderdale," the old man said, staring at the canvas bag in James's hand.

"Sounds good," James told him.

James hurried around the front of the car, pulled open the passenger's door, and lowered himself into the leather seat.

"What's your name?" the old man asked, easing the car back onto the road.

"George," James told him. "George Murphy."

James rested his head against the cool seatback and studied the old man, driving with both hands tight on top of the wheel.

"Nice car," James said, rubbing his open palm over the seat.

Guess this is my lucky night, he thought.

Chapter 2

"Christina — slow down!"

Terri slumped lower in the passenger seat and raised her knees to the dashboard. "Please — slow down!"

Christina, her dark eyes glowing with mischief, ignored her friend. Instead, she pressed her sandal on the gas pedal, and the Honda Accord surged forward with a roar.

"Christina!" Terri pleaded.

"I'm just so tired of going fifteen everywhere!" Christina exclaimed, swerving past a rumbling gasoline truck, then cutting back into the right lane. "Everyone in Florida drives fifteen miles an hour. It just makes me crazy!"

"We don't want to get stopped," Terri said softly. "You know that."

Christina took a hand off the wheel and brushed it back through her blonde corkscrew curls. "Hey — we came to Florida to live dangerously, right? Have a little fun?"

"You've had plenty of fun already," Terri said

dryly with a hint of disapproval in her voice. "You haven't stopped partying since the moment we arrived."

Christina's face broke into a broad grin. "What was the name of that boy?" she asked.

"Which boy?"

"The real hunky one," Christina replied, still grinning.

"*Which* real hunky one?" Terri cried.

Both girls laughed.

"You didn't do so bad, either," Christina told her friend, speeding up to pass a Greyhound bus.

"Do you think Matthew will write to me?" Terri asked, staring out the window as the trees whirred by in the afternoon sunlight.

"Does he know how to write?" Christina joked.

"He knows more than you might think," Terri said slyly.

"What a week!" Christina exclaimed. "What an *awesome* week."

"I even got some swimming in," Terri said.

"You're an *awesome* swimmer," Christina exclaimed. "I knew you were good, but — "

"I can't believe it's over already, and we have to go back," Terri moaned.

And then her expression turned serious as she glanced at something moving in the mirror outside the passenger door. "Slow down, Christina. *Now.* Is that a cop?"

Christina's expression changed, too, as she raised her eyes to the mirror. She hit the brakes,

and the car responded. "No. It's just a tow truck."
She exhaled loudly, relieved.

"I saw the flashing lights — " Terri said.

"Just a tow truck," Christina repeated.

"If we get stopped — " Terri started.

"Don't worry," Christina interrupted. "I can't believe I'm friends with such a worrier."

"Someone has to worry," Terri said softly.

The two friends, both seventeen, their birthdays just three weeks apart, were as different in appearance as they were in temperament.

Christina was thin, almost wiry, with blonde corkscrew curls piled on her head. She had dramatic, dark brown eyes, playful eyes on a mischievous face. Her mouth seemed to fall naturally into a teasing smile. She always appeared to be enjoying some private joke.

Terri was as cautious as her friend was impulsive and playful. She had sky-blue eyes and creamy white skin, which looked even paler against her straight black hair, which she wore swept back, falling down to her shoulders.

Also in contrast to Christina and her boyish figure, Terri was chubby. "Full-bodied." That's how her mother described her. Terri worried about her size a lot, although she chose not to discuss it with Christina.

Christina would tell me I'm exaggerating. Or she'd just make a joke, she decided.

And to Terri, it was no joking matter.

"How long are we going to stay in Tampa?" Terri asked.

Christina shrugged her slender shoulders. She was wearing an oversized chartreuse T-shirt over green spandex bicycle shorts. "Who knows? I just want to see if I can find that boy I met last year."

"The football player?"

Christina nodded, her eyes on the road.

"Isn't he a little *old* for you?" Terri asked, shaking her head.

Christina laughed. "You're such a worrier, *mom*."

"Stop — "

"He thinks I'm twenty-one," Christina said, chuckling.

"You don't look twenty-one," Terri told her. She sighed impatiently. "You know, we've had more than enough excitement on this trip. Maybe we should just chill and head for home."

"He might not even be there," Christina replied, as if that answered Terri. "Maybe he moved or something. I haven't heard from him in months."

"It's getting awfully hot in here," Terri complained. "Can you turn up the air conditioner?"

Christina glanced down at the dashboard controls. "I don't think I know how. *You* do it."

Terri studied the dials in front of her. She slid one forward all the way. It didn't seem to make any difference. "Why do they make it so confusing?"

"Should we trade it in for an American car?" Christina joked.

She turned up the radio. A road sign proclaiming Highway 84 whirred by in a blur. The bright afternoon sun poured in through the windshield. It had rained the day before. All the trees and tall grass were still glistening, sparkling in the bright light.

Unreal, Terri thought.

Everything about this trip has been unreal.

"The beach was so crowded," Christina complained. "Remember Josh?"

"The rich one with the bandanna?"

"No. That was Eric," Christina said, laughing. "Josh was kind of short. . . ."

"Kind of short? He came up to your waist!" Terri exclaimed.

"Sometimes good things come in small packages," Christina said dryly.

"Christina, he was a total wimp," Terri insisted.

"Not *total*," Christina said.

Both girls laughed.

"Well, what about him?" Terri asked impatiently.

"I forget."

More easy laughter.

"It was too crowded. That's what I started to say," Christina told her friend. She swerved to pass a slow-moving stationwagon loaded down with lumber that stuck out the back window.

"Maybe we should go to Daytona next time," Terri suggested, opening the glove compartment, searching its contents.

"Yuck. No way," Christina exclaimed. "It's all high school geeks." She made a disgusted face. "And it's more crowded than Lauderdale."

"Well, how about Palm Beach?"

"Too many rich snobs," Christina replied. "They

all live in compounds. None of them have just a house."

"Sounds good to me," Terri said.

"What are you looking for in there?" Christina asked, taking her eyes off the road to stare at Terri, who was still pawing through the glove compartment.

"Just looking." Terri shoved it shut. She glanced outside. "Kind of swampy out there."

"What do you expect?" Christina snapped. "This whole state is a swamp. Except for the beach."

"I love Florida," Terri said.

Christina turned to look at her friend. "You even got a tan. You're always so pale. I didn't think you *could* tan."

Terri started to reply. But her mouth dropped open in horror as she saw the enormous red truck roaring toward them. She saw it — and then realized that Christina didn't.

"*Look out!*" Terri managed to scream.

Christina swerved, but too late.

The crash was deafening.

Chapter 3

"Christina — we should stop."

Terri turned, peering through the rear window at the truck.

"We *can't* stop!" Christina exclaimed, pushing the gas pedal to the floor. The car roared forward obediently.

"But the driver — he might be hurt. He slammed right into that concrete embankment."

"He's okay," Christina said calmly, eyes straight ahead, her features set. "He's a truck driver, Terri. He'll radio for help if he needs it."

"But what if he's really hurt?" Terri insisted. "I mean, we *made* him crash."

"No, we didn't," Christina replied softly. "Terri, you know we can't stop. We don't want to get in trouble, do we?"

"I — I don't believe you. You're so — *calm*!" Terri exclaimed, turning back to the front, readjusting her seat belt.

"He's fine," Christina insisted, glancing in the

outside mirror. "I can see him. He's outside the truck. He's okay."

"The crash was so loud," Terri said, wrapping her arms around her chest as if shielding herself. "I was sure we were hit."

"Take a deep breath," her friend said.

"What good will *that* do?" Terri asked, her voice shrill and high-pitched.

Christina shrugged. "I don't know. Sounded like a good idea."

"How can you make jokes? We were almost killed!"

"Well, we're okay now," Christina said, glancing in the mirror, slowing the car to sixty.

"What if he memorized our license number?" Terri fretted.

Christina laughed. "He was too busy crashing to memorize any license numbers."

Terri slumped down in the seat. "I feel sick."

"Just chill, will you? We're okay. Let's not spoil the whole vacation because some truck driver was in the wrong lane."

"But *you* were in the wrong lane," Terri insisted.

"Whatever," Christina muttered.

They drove on for a while in silence. Terri closed her eyes and tried to force the sound of the crash, the squeal and crunch of metal, out of her head.

"So you really liked that guy Matthew?" Christina asked after a while.

Terri opened her eyes and glanced at the speedometer. Fifty-five. Well, she thought, at least the accident has caused Christina to slow down.

"Yeah. He was kind of nice," she answered distractedly. "But he was a little too eager, if you know what I mean."

Christina chuckled. "I like 'em eager."

Terri frowned. "No. There was something *too* eager about him. I mean . . . well . . . I don't know what I mean."

"He frightened you?" Christina asked, her expression amused.

"No. Well. Yeah."

Christina laughed.

"Are you laughing at me?" Terri asked, hurt.

"No. Of course not," Christina insisted. "You just seem so . . . confused."

"Remember that party on the beach the first night?" Terri recollected, staring out her window. A clump of low weeping willows slumped over the highway. "Everyone was drinking beer and the music was so loud? Well, Matthew pulled me away from the party, and we — "

"Hey, look at that hitchhiker," Christina interrupted. She slowed the car.

"Oh, no!" Terri declared firmly. "No way. No way, Christina."

"Huh?"

"No way we're picking up a hitchhiker. Haven't we done enough?"

"Enough is never enough," Christina said, her dark eyes glowing with excitement.

"Don't stop! I mean it!" Terri insisted.

"But look how cute he is," Christina said, braking hard.

"Cute? He looks like a killer!"

"Don't exaggerate, *mom*," Christina said, sticking her tongue out at her friend.

"Stop calling me mom. I really hate it."

"Then stop acting like mom," Christina said sharply. She pulled the car to the shoulder of the highway.

The hitchhiker shifted the canvas bag he was carrying and came trotting up to Terri's side of the car. He had short blond hair, Terri saw, and startling green eyes. And he was big, muscular, like a jock, and very broad-shouldered.

"Christina — I don't like this," Terri said unhappily.

Christina laughed at her. "What could happen?"

Chapter 4

James tossed his bag into the back seat of the Accord and then slid in after it. "Don't you girls know you should never pick up a hitchhiker?" he asked, smiling so they would know he was joking.

They both laughed, nervous laughs.

"What's your name?" the blonde one with all the hair asked, turning to examine him.

"James," he told her. "James Dark."

Whoa, he thought. I messed up. I usually lie and give a phony name. Just for fun. Why did I tell her my real name?

"Do people call you Jim?" the other one, the chubby one, asked him. She was tugging nervously at a strand of her black hair, watching him in the rearview mirror.

"No. No one calls me Jim," he told her. He shrugged. "No reason. Everyone's just always called me James."

The blonde one introduced herself and her friend. Christina Jenkins and Terri Martin. James said their names over and over in his head, his way of memorizing. Christina and Terri. Christina and Terri.

They're both pretty hot, he thought, settling back on the seat, rubbing his open palm against the upholstery. "Pretty humid out there," he said, smiling.

I wish Christina would stop staring at me like that. She's starting to make me nervous.

"Where are you headed?" Christina asked him.

James shrugged. "Doesn't really matter. Just *away*."

"We're going to Tampa," Terri said, glancing nervously at Christina.

"Hey, I've got a cousin in Tampa," James said. "My cousin Paul. And come to think of it, he owes me money."

"Excellent," Christina said. "So we can drop you off there."

"Excellent," James repeated. "Where are you going after Tampa?"

"Home," Terri answered quickly.

"Where's home?" James asked.

"Well . . . Cleveland," Terri replied reluctantly, glancing again at Christina.

"You two live in Cleveland?" James exclaimed. "I didn't think *anyone* lived in Cleveland."

"You can't exactly call it *living*," Christina joked.

They all laughed.

Christina pulled the car back onto the highway. Terri fiddled with her seat belt.

Not bad, James thought.

I could go for either one.

Maybe both.

Maybe I'll let them take me all the way to Cleveland. Wow. Talk about changes. Cleveland has *got* to be different from Key West. Like the difference between Earth and Mars!

"It's all swamp out there," he said, gazing out the window.

"All the rain has made it even swampier," Terri said.

"Where are you from?" Christina asked.

"Key West," James replied, then silently scolded himself for telling the truth again. "You two on vacation?" He wanted to keep the conversation away from him. He had already told them too much.

"Yeah. School break," Christina offered. "You go to school in Key West?"

"Not too often," he replied, grinning.

They both laughed.

"You been to Disney World?" he asked, rubbing his hand over the smooth seat cushion.

"No way," Christina replied. "We like the beach. We came down to party. You know. Not walk around in mouse ears."

James snickered. "Where'd you go? Miami?"

"No. Lauderdale," Christina said, speeding up to pass a family camper being pulled by an old Plymouth filled with kids.

"You have a good time?" James asked.

"Excellent," Christina said.

"You're the quiet one?" James asked, leaning forward to get Terri's attention.

"Yeah. That's me," Terri replied dryly.

"You look like a girl I used to know," he said.

"Really?" Terri asked without interest.

"Yeah. Her name was Lizzy. She was a great swimmer. Used to dive, too. Used to go diving with those treasure hunters. You know. The ones who found that old ship buried by the reef. You look a lot like her."

"I'm a pretty good swimmer, too. Are you on vacation?" Terri asked uncomfortably.

"Not really," James said.

"You're not on vacation, and you don't really know where you're going?" Christina asked.

"That sums it up pretty well," James said, grinning at her as she peered into the rearview mirror at him.

"And you hitchhiked up here from Key West?" Terri asked.

"Like to ask a lot of questions?" James shot back.

He saw Terri's face turn bright scarlet.

Whoa, he told himself. Cool it with the sarcasm, man. These girls are going to take you all the way to Cleveland. You don't want to make them nervous.

He laughed to show Terri he was joking. "I was lucky. I got all the way up to Lauderdale in one ride," he told her.

They drove on for a while in silence. The late afternoon sun poured in through the windshield. Waves of heat rose up from the road, making it appear to sizzle and bubble.

James tapped his fingers nervously on the seat,

then fiddled with the handle of his canvas bag. He didn't like silence.

Silence always gave him bad thoughts.

Silence gave him too much time to think.

Once again, he heard her voice, pleading with him, begging him not to hurt her.

She's following me, he thought.

She's going to follow me all the way to Cleveland.

"Can't you turn up the air conditioner?" he asked, leaning into the front seat. "It's pretty hot back here."

"I tried to," Terri said, reaching again for the controls. "But I'm not sure how."

James leaned forward a little more and studied the dials. "Push up the one marked 'Fan,'" he told Terri. "That'll make it blow more."

It took her a while to find it. Then she obediently pushed it to Maximum, and cold air began blowing from the vents.

"You're a genius!" Christina proclaimed.

"That's what everyone says," James replied. He settled back in the seat, enjoying the feel of the cool air on his face.

They drove on in silence. The sun hovered low above the uncurving highway. It looked as if they were going to drive right into it.

"Hey — anybody hungry?" James asked after a while, mostly to break the silence. The painful silence. "There's a cool-looking diner over there."

Christina slowed the car. They turned their eyes to the diner, set off the road behind a narrow gravel parking lot. It looked like a railroad car, all shiny metal with a single row of windows along the length of it. A neon sign perched above the flat roof hadn't been turned on yet. It proclaimed EVERGLADES DINER in big block letters.

"Let's try it," Christina said and made a sharp turn into the narrow lot.

"The Everglades isn't near here," Terri protested.

"Maybe Mr. Everglade owns the place," Christina joked.

James laughed. "Maybe they serve alligator burgers."

Christina parked the car by the front entrance and cut the engine.

"Aren't alligators endangered?" Terri asked.

"Aren't we all?" James said dryly. He climbed out of the car and stretched his legs, reaching his hands high above his head. Out of the corner of his eye, he saw both girls watching him.

They're both hot for me, he thought, secretly pleased.

This could be an interesting ride.

"You work out?" Christina asked him. Their shoes crunched over the gravel as they made their way to the glass front door of the diner.

"A little," James said modestly.

He stared at her, giving her his sexiest smile. He expected her to look away, but she stared right back at him.

It was cool inside the diner. The roar of the air conditioner competed with the country music on the jukebox.

A young man in a white apron stood behind the counter, silently moving his lips as he read a copy of the *National Enquirer*. He had spikey brown hair, a face full of pimples, and a diamond stud in one ear. He looked up for a second as James and the girls entered, then quickly returned his eyes to his newspaper.

James led the way to a red vinyl booth at the end. They were the only customers, he saw. The two girls slid in across from him.

"Who's that singing?" Christina asked.

"Randy Travis," James told her.

"Is he supposed to be good?" she asked, picking up a plastic menu.

James's mouth dropped open. "Huh? You don't know Randy Travis?"

"I'm not into country," Christina replied, studying the menu.

"I think I saw him on TV once," Terri remarked.

"You're missing a lot," James told them seriously. He'd been listening to country music his whole life. He liked it because it was so sad. Just about every song was sad in some way. Even the singers' voices were sad.

They studied the menu. James kept glancing up at Christina and Terri.

Two hot babes, he thought.

Hope I can keep out of trouble.

But bad luck and trouble are my middle names.

Hey, that's a country song, I think.

Bad luck and trouble.

Who sang it? Should be my theme song. . . .

He tossed the menu onto the scratched Formica tabletop. Turning his head, he called to the guy behind the counter. "Hey — can we get some service? You're not too busy, are you?"

The young man didn't react at all. He continued to read his paper, moving his lips as he read.

James could feel his anger start to build.

It always started in his chest, a heavy burning feeling. He could feel his chest tighten. Then the anger spread to his neck muscles. Then he felt the familiar throbbing at his temples.

After a long while, the counter boy looked up, slowly folded the paper in half, made his way around the counter, and ambled down the row of booths to where James and his companions were sitting.

"Hey — you're a real go-getter," James said sarcastically. "You really ought to slow down, you know."

The young man ignored James and stared at the two girls. "You ready to order?" he asked them.

"We've *been* ready," James snapped angrily.

He continued to ignore James, his eyes concentrating on Christina. "Hey, you're not too shabby-looking," he said, a lopsided smile forming on his pocked face.

"Do you like those teeth?" James asked him, his green eyes narrowing into menacing slits. "Or should I remove them for you?"

The young man's nostrils flared as he turned to James. He tapped James on the shoulder with one finger. "Listen, man — "

James exploded.

As he had so many times before.

He leapt to his feet and grabbed the startled kid's apron front with both hands.

"Hey — *don't*!" James heard Terri yell.

Too late.

James gave the guy a hard, two-handed shove that sent him sprawling backwards across the aisle. His back hit the counter hard, and he cried out in pain.

"James — what are you *doing*?" Terri was screaming. "He didn't do anything to you!"

But James felt the blood throbbing at his temples. Felt the red anger tighten his chest.

"Hey, man — " The guy raised both hands as if to shield himself, but James grabbed him again, pulled him away from the counter, then slammed him hard again. This time, he seemed to bounce off the counter, crying out as he hit, then slumping to his knees on the dirty floor.

"*James!*" Terri was screaming.

"Come on. We're outta here," James said, glaring down at the counter boy, who made no attempt to get to his feet.

"But *James!*"

They followed him out of the diner, back onto the gravel parking lot. The sun was dipping behind the cypress trees across the highway.

He could see the two girls casting meaningful glances at each other.

Were they frightened — or impressed?

Terri definitely looked frightened. He couldn't read Christina's expression.

"What a creep," James muttered, kicking a clump of gravel across the lot. "I mean. Really. What a creep."

"But, James — " Terri started, her eyes on Christina.

James giggled for some reason. A high-pitched giggle. It just escaped from him like air whooshing out of a balloon.

The anger had followed him out of the diner, but he was beginning to calm down. The throbbing in his head stopped. His neck muscles began to relax.

"You've got quite a temper," Christina said, eyeing him intently, as if seeing him for the first time.

You don't know the half of it, girl, James thought.

You don't know the half of it.

Chapter 5

"I think we made a bad mistake," Terri whispered. "I *told* you not to pick him up."

She peered into the rearview mirror and watched James, sound asleep in the back seat, shadows flickering over his face, head resting on the window frame, his mouth open slightly.

"He looks like a little boy when he's asleep," Christina whispered, turning in the passenger seat to look at him. She turned back to Terri.

"Freddie Kreuger's little boy," Terri muttered, returning her eyes to the road. Night had fallen so suddenly, like a curtain being dropped. The blue-black sky seemed to hover low and heavy. The darkness somehow felt *thick*. "He practically *killed* that counter boy for no reason at all."

"Ssshhh," Christina warned. "You'll wake him up."

"So what?" Terri snapped. "He's been sleeping since Sarasota. Maybe he could wake up and drive for a while. My eyes are really tired."

"Well, don't exaggerate," Christina whispered.

"He didn't practically kill that kid in the diner. He only pushed him."

"Yeah. Right," Terri said sarcastically, rolling her eyes.

A sign proclaiming Highway 75 popped into the white glare of their headlights. The road curved, and a dark expanse, darker than the road, darker than the trees, came into view, an endless black hole seemingly stretching forever.

"Is that water?" Christina asked, still whispering.

"Yeah. The Gulf," Terri replied. "We're getting pretty close to Tampa Bay, I think. I can't wait to drop him off in Tampa."

"But he's so cute," Christina protested. "He's just a big teddy bear."

"A teddy bear with a temper," Terri whispered. "He's scary, Christina."

"Maybe that's what I like about him," Christina said thoughtfully. She turned to stare into the back seat at him again.

James moaned in his sleep and shifted his position.

"He's running away from something," Terri whispered. "Something bad. I can tell."

"Stop being so melodramatic," Christina scolded, shaking her head. "I told you, you've been watching *General Hospital* too long. Life isn't a soap, Terri."

"Then why wouldn't he tell us where he's going?" Terri demanded. "Or whether he's in school or not. Or anything. He wouldn't tell us anything about himself."

"He's just shy," Christina replied. And then she poked Terri playfully in the side. "Come on. Admit it. You think he's cute, too."

"No way," Terri insisted. "And don't poke me while I'm driving."

"Wow," Christina said softly. "Wow. You're certainly touchy all of a sudden."

"I'm frightened, that's all," Terri replied heatedly. "Things have gone okay up till now. I mean, considering. But we didn't need him to complicate things. For all we know, he's a total psycho!"

"Did someone say psycho?"

The voice from the back seat made Christina and Terri cry out.

James laughed. "What's going on? Where are we?" He pulled himself up straight and rubbed his eyes. "Is this Cleveland?"

"Ha-ha," said Christina sarcastically. "You slept a long time. But not that long. We're about eighty miles from Tampa."

"Great," James said, scratching his head. "I hope you two were talking about me while I was asleep."

"Actually, we were," Christina confessed.

Terri glared at her angrily.

"Did you decide I was a *baaad* dude?" James asked playfully.

"The baddest," Christina quickly replied, turning in the passenger seat to smile at him. "Want to drive for a bit? Terri's getting a little sleepy."

"Yeah. Sure." James sounded surprised.

"Do you have a license?" Terri asked suspiciously.

"A fishing license?" he joked.

"That'll do," Christina said. "I only have a temporary, which is no good in Florida. But I've done most of the driving." She shot a meaningful glance at Terri.

"You're a real criminal," James said, snickering. "I'm impressed."

Christina and Terri exchanged quick glances again.

Terri pulled the car to the side of the highway and put it in park. She pushed open her door and climbed out. A wave of hot, wet air floated into the car.

James slid behind the wheel, smiling at Christina, his green eyes flashing in the yellow light from the ceiling as Terri settled into the back seat. He reached down to the bottom of the seat, found the lever after a brief search, and pushed the seat back to make room for his legs. Then, a few seconds later, they were moving again, gliding through the inky night on the nearly deserted highway.

Christina studied him as he drove. She liked his serious expression. The way he chewed on his lower lip as he narrowed his eyes to the windshield. The way his blond hair seemed to sparkle in the light of oncoming cars.

He's really handsome, she thought. In a hard sort of way.

In a dangerous sort of way.

"It's so quiet," James said uncomfortably, drumming his fingers on the wheel. "Let's see if we can get anything on the radio."

He removed his right hand from the wheel and reached for the radio dial.

But before he could locate it, they heard the siren.

Loud. And close.

Wailing like a howling animal right behind them.

And then the flashing red lights reflected in the rearview mirror, filling the car with a frightening, pulsating pink glow.

"Cops!" James cried. "But I'm not speeding!"

"I *knew* it!" Terri cried shrilly from the back seat. "We never should've picked him up! I *knew* it!"

Christina cast an accusing glance at James. "Don't try anything! Just pull over!" she shouted over the wailing of the siren.

Chapter 6

"I knew it!" Terri cried, turning to stare out of the back window into the pulsating red lights.

"Shut up! Shut up!" Christina screamed, holding her hands over her ears.

The car bumped onto the shoulder of the highway, kicking up gravel, then bounced through tall weeds.

This isn't happening, Christina thought, closing her eyes, trying to shut out the steady siren howl, trying to shut out the world.

But the siren grew louder.

And then the red lights that seemed to bounce through the car faded. The car grew dark again.

And the siren faded, too.

They watched in stunned silence as the police car sped past.

In seconds, it had disappeared around the curve of the highway. The red taillights were there, tiny red eyes moving against the darkness. And then they were gone.

Silence. Dark silence.

"He's probably just going home to dinner," James said and laughed loudly, shaking his head.

The girls didn't laugh.

Finally, Christina pulled herself up in the passenger seat. "Guess we panicked a little," she said dryly. She turned back to Terri. "You okay?"

Terri nodded. "Yeah. Fine," she replied with some bitterness. "I thought — "

James put an arm on the seatback and turned to face Terri. "I heard what you said," he told her softly, his smile fading quickly.

"I . . . I didn't mean . . ." Terri started, then looked to Christina for help.

"Do you think I'm wanted or something?" James asked her, sounding hurt. His eyes peered intently into hers. "Think I'm some kind of dangerous criminal?"

"No," Terri replied quickly. "I was just afraid." She turned her eyes to Christina. "Back at the diner, you seemed so . . . out of control."

"So you thought the police were after me?" James demanded.

"Yes. No. I don't know *what* I was thinking. I was just scared," Terri confessed. And then she added, "I'm sorry. I apologize. Okay?"

"Okay." James extended his hand and shook hands with her.

Terri was surprised to find that his hand was ice cold.

Was James more frightened of being stopped by the police than he was willing to let on?

"Wow. I was sure you were speeding or something," Christina said. She put a hand on James's broad shoulder, then quickly removed it. "How fast were you going?"

"Not very fast," he said, turning back to the wheel, glancing in the rearview mirror. "Only about fifty." He shifted into drive and rolled the car off the tall grass of the shoulder, onto the highway.

"On to Tampa!" Christina declared brightly. "And if another cop chases after us, we'll give him a race — right?"

James laughed. "Right. We'll just throw the car into *turbo* and bomb away from him!"

He lowered his foot on the gas, and the car sped into the night. Christina watched the needle on the speedometer rise. It leveled off at sixty.

"How fast do you think this car can go?" she asked.

"Not very," James replied, his face hidden in shadow.

"What's the fastest you've ever driven?" she asked him, moving closer to him, studying his face again as it moved in and out of shadow.

"I haven't driven much," he told her seriously. "My aunt can't afford a car."

Christina clicked her tongue. She placed her hand on his shoulder again, testing him. He didn't seem to mind, so she left it there for a while. "Poor boy," she said with mock sympathy.

"I hope you're not making fun of me," he said playfully, taking his eyes off the road long enough to glance at her.

"Who me?" Christina turned to the back. Terri

was sitting straight up, but her head had fallen forward. Her slow, heavy breathing indicated that she was asleep.

Christina let her hair brush against James's shoulder. He pretended not to notice.

She felt drawn to him, as if being pulled in by a powerful force. He was so different from the boys she had partied with all week at the beach. He was so serious . . . so solid . . . so mysterious.

The other boys were all such lightweights. They were only interested in partying and surfing and getting girls.

But James — James was interested in . . .

She didn't know *what* James was interested in.

She didn't know a thing about him. Not a thing.

She yawned and closed her eyes. "James, are you a mystery?" she blurted out.

I must be tired, she thought. I'd never say anything like that if I were fully awake.

"I'm a mystery waiting to be solved," he said. She opened her eyes to find him grinning at her.

He took his right hand from the wheel. Christina thought he was going to hold her hand. But instead he reached for the radio dial and clicked it on.

A preacher's voice boomed through the car. James turned down the volume.

Christina arched her neck to see if it had awakened Terri. She was still asleep, her chin still lowered to her chest.

James pushed the buttons till he found a soft rock station. James Taylor's voice filled the car.

Christina let her hair brush lightly against James's shoulder again.

The music ended. An announcer's voice came on, reading a commercial for a used car lot in Bradenton.

The highway dipped, then continued straight north along the coast. The deep, dark Gulf of Mexico was out of view now. But it was there, just beyond the silent trees.

"And now a K-107 news update," said the voice with just a hint of southern accent. "Earlier today, an elderly Fort Lauderdale man was found unconscious beside Highway 95 just south of the city. His name is being withheld at this time pending notification of his kin.

"Police report that he was beaten with a blunt object and dragged from his car. The car was stolen. At this time, Fort Lauderdale police believe that a hitchhiker may be responsible — "

James clicked off the radio.

He turned to Christina with a troubled expression. "I hate news — don't you?" he asked very softly.

Chapter 7

"I think that's my cousin's house there," James said, pointing. "No. Maybe not."

"How can you tell one from another?" Christina asked, yawning. "The houses all look exactly alike."

Terri slowed the car. They were driving through a development of square, white stucco, Spanish-style houses, set close together, one right after the other, on small squares of lawn.

"I think Paul's house is number forty-two," James said, squinting at the stenciled numbers on the mailboxes. "That's what I remember. Forty-two. I was here last year sometime."

"We've circled this block twice," Terri said impatiently.

"Circle it one more time," James instructed. "I'm pretty sure I know which one it is."

Terri sighed wearily.

It seemed as if they'd been driving forever. Now they were irritable, blinking in the bright sunlight, yawning, impatient to find their destination.

They think I'm staying at my cousin's, James

thought, shielding his eyes with one hand as he squinted at the passing mailboxes.

They're in for a surprise.

He had made his decision. He was going to ride all the way to Cleveland with them.

The farther away, the better, he decided.

Maybe Cleveland isn't far enough.

He knew Christina would be pleased. He could tell that she was interested in him. The way she stared so intensely into his eyes. The way she studied him. The way she let her hair brush his shoulder, trying to make it seem so casual. The way she kept touching him, putting her hand on his arm as she talked.

She's definitely hot for me, James told himself, pleased.

We'll have a nice long car ride to get to know each other better. Christina won't be at all unhappy about my decision to come with them.

He wasn't so sure about Terri.

Terri still treated him coldly, suspiciously. He caught the unhappy glances she kept throwing to Christina.

And he remembered what Terri had said: "We never should've picked him up."

No, Terri wasn't exactly his friend.

She seemed so nervous. More than nervous — frightened.

James snickered to himself. She's afraid of Big Bad James.

Well, good. Maybe she'll be too frightened to

make a fuss when I announce that I'm riding to Cleveland with them.

He suddenly felt hot, uncomfortable. Itchy. He scratched the back of his neck and discovered a big mosquito bite there. How do mosquitoes get in the car, anyway? he wondered, annoyed.

"There. Forty-two. Pull up the drive," he told Terri.

The two-story, white stucco house looked like all the others in the neighborhood. For some reason, there was a lawn rake resting on the slanted, red tile roof. In the middle of the small front yard, a lawn sprinkler was sending up a circular spray. A child's tricycle on the grass near the driveway was receiving a good shower.

A gray Toyota Corolla stood half in, half out of the narrow garage to the right of the house. A red plastic whiffle bat and a large, white ball lay on the driveway in front of the car.

"Your cousin has a kid?" Christina asked, running a hand through her hair, trying to fluff it up.

"Yeah. A little boy," James told her, staring up at the open front door. "Name's Ethan. He's cool."

"I've got to get something to eat," Terri moaned. She cut the engine and pushed open her door.

"At least you had a little sleep last night," Christina told her, still working at her hair. "I was up all night."

"Me, too," James said, pushing open the back door, shielding his eyes from the white glare of sunlight. "I'm sure Paul will let us crash here tonight."

"What's his wife's name?" Terri asked, stretching

her arms and legs and then trying to smooth out her wrinkled T-shirt.

"Paula," James replied.

"Paul and Paula?" Christina exclaimed.

James laughed. "Yeah."

"Cute," Christina said, making a face.

"She's okay," James said, not meaning it to sound as defensive as it did.

"It's so hot," Terri complained. "Why doesn't someone plant some trees out here? It's like a desert!"

"It's a new development," James said. And then, impulsively, he said, "You want to cool off?"

Terri gave him a suspicious look. "Yeah. Why?"

"No problem," he replied, grinning. He grabbed her shoulders from behind and began pushing her toward the sprinkler.

"Hey — get off!" Terri cried angrily.

She tried to pull back, but he was a lot stronger.

"Get off, James! Let *go*!"

But he pushed until they were both under the sprinkler.

Terri shrieked as the cold water showered her.

Laughing, James let go. He raised his face to the cold water.

Slipping on the wet grass, Terri ran back to the driveway. She turned and shook a fist at him. "You creep!"

"Don't you feel cooler?" he asked, grinning at her, letting the water soak through his shirt.

"What's going on out here?" a man's voice called.

James turned his eyes to the front stoop. "Hey — Paul!"

The young man let the screen door slam behind him. "James — is that you?"

"Come on out. We're having a party!" James declared.

"Same old James," Paul said, shaking his head. Then he noticed Christina and Terri standing in the driveway. "Hi. You with him?"

They nodded. Terri was trying to shake the water from her hair.

Completely drenched, James hurried over to Paul and shook his hand. "Hey, you look great, Paul."

"Thanks, man. You look *terrible*."

They both laughed.

Paul was tall and lanky. He wore a sleeveless blue T-shirt over white tennis shorts. He was in his late twenties, but his hair had already started to thin, leaving a wide forehead over his lively, blue eyes. The tight T-shirt revealed the beginnings of a potbelly.

James introduced Christina and Terri.

Paul nodded to them, then turned back to James, a wide grin on his face. "Not bad. Not bad, man. Maybe I'll come with *you*!"

Paul slapped James a high-five. The girls laughed. Uncomfortable laughter.

"Could we get out of the sun?" Christina asked. "It's pretty hot out here."

"Yeah. Of course," Paul said. "Come on in." He gestured to the front door, then turned back to

James. "Paula will sure be surprised."

All four of them started toward the house. Paul stopped and put a hand on James's wet shoulder. His expression turned serious. "You been keeping out of trouble, man?"

"Yeah. Sure," James replied uncomfortably. He glanced at the two girls. They were staring at him and Paul.

"No. Really," Paul insisted, not taking his hand off James's shoulder. "You keeping out of trouble?"

"Yeah. I *said* yeah," James snapped. He pushed Paul's hand away. "What do you want from me?" He saw the girls turn to each other and flash each other meaningful glances.

"I just want to hear that you're keeping out of trouble," Paul said, taking long strides to keep up with James as James made his way quickly to the front door.

"You're not my father," James said sharply. He hadn't meant it to come out sounding so angry. Why was he losing his temper at Paul already? He knew Paul didn't mean anything by it.

He's embarrassing me in front of them, James thought, turning to look back at the girls.

He's deliberately embarrassing me.

That's why I got angry.

Just chill, he warned himself. Paul's a good guy. He just never knows when to keep his mouth shut.

Paul held the screen door open, and James and the girls made their way into the house. It wasn't much cooler inside. A fan on an end table beside a low couch blew hot air at them as they stepped into the small living room.

"Hey, Paula! Paula!" Paul called. "Come see who's here. We've got company!"

Paula emerged from the kitchen, drying her hands on a checkered dish towel. Her mouth dropped open in surprise when she saw James.

She's as mousey as ever, he thought. Paula was short and thin, with frizzy brown hair piled up on her head. Her small face was made even smaller by the oversized pink plastic eyeglasses she wore.

"James — you're soaking wet!" she exclaimed in greeting.

He smiled. "Yeah. Terri and I . . . uh . . . went for a swim."

Paula playfully tossed the dish towel at him.

Ethan came toddling into the room. He was about four, chubby, roundfaced, and very blond. "Who are *they*?" he asked his mom, pointing a water pistol at the new arrivals.

"See? Didn't I bring him up to be polite?" Paula joked. She pointed to James. "Ethan, don't you remember your cousin James? Remember he was here last year?"

"No," Ethan replied, keeping the plastic pistol trained on James.

"Sure, you remember him, Ethan," Paul said, grinning at James.

"No, I don't," Ethan insisted. He stared hard at James. "Did you go in the sprinkler?"

"Yeah," James replied.

"Dad said we're not allowed," Ethan declared.

James laughed. "Sorry. Guess I'm in trouble."

"When are you *not*?" Paula said.

James started to respond, but Paul interrupted. "Paula, let's get these guys something to eat and drink. From the looks of them, they've been on the road a long time."

The day passed pleasantly. James was glad he'd decided to stop. Everyone's very relaxed, he thought. Several times he looked up to see Christina smiling at him warmly.

They had an early dinner. Some pretty good fried chicken, mashed potatoes, ice cream for dessert.

Paula insisted on their spending the night. It would be a little crowded, but they could manage. Christina and Terri would sleep on cots in the guest room. James would get the living room couch.

After dinner, James and Paul talked in the dining room. The TV blared in the living room. Ethan was watching Bugs Bunny cartoons, calling for everyone to join him.

James began to feel tense, felt his neck muscles tighten, his mouth go dry, as he prepared to ask Paul for the money Paul owed him.

It had been such a nice, relaxing day. No tension at all. James hated to spoil it.

But if he was heading off to Cleveland, he needed the money.

"Hey, Paul," he started, trying to sound casual. He rubbed a hand back through his short blond hair.

"I know what you're going to say," Paul interrupted, leaning over the table, still filled with dirty dinner dishes, twirling his silver wedding band with his right hand.

"Oh, yeah?" James replied. "What?"

"You're going to ask if I'd be willing to take one of the girls off your hands."

They both laughed.

"No way," James said. He glanced through the doorway into the living room. Christina and Terri were seated on the couch with Ethan between them, watching the cartoons.

James cleared his throat and started again. "It's about the money you owe me."

"Hey, no problem," Paul said. He jumped to his feet. "Come here. I'll give it to you now. Fifty bucks, right?"

Surprised and relieved, James followed Paul into the living room. Paul led him across the room to a narrow counter in the front entry that held his car keys, some spare change, and his wallet.

"Wow. That wallet is bulging!" James exlaimed.

With a wide grin on his face, Paul unfolded the wallet and pulled out a thick stack of bills. "Ssshhhh." He raised a finger to his lips.

"Where'd you get that kind of money?" James whispered, staring as Paul pulled out a fifty-dollar bill and handed it to him.

"I did a little favor for the boss," Paul told him, still grinning.

"What *kind* of favor?" James demanded.

Again, Paul raised his finger to his lips. He didn't answer. "A little favor, that's all. So I got a bonus. You ever see a thousand dollars in fifties before?"

He held the wad of money in front of James's nose. "Go ahead. Sniff it. It's real. A thousand bucks."

"Wow, that's great, Paul," James whispered. He tucked the fifty into his jeans pocket. "You did good."

"Tell me about it," Paul said quietly. He folded the money back into the wallet and tossed the wallet onto the counter.

James followed him into the living room.

The cartoons had gone off. A local news program had come on.

"I want more cartoons," Ethan demanded. "Put on a tape, Dad."

"Roger Eckridge, the Fort Lauderdale man found unconscious on Route 95 last night, remains in a coma, hanging on to life at Fort Lauderdale General today," the newsman said, reading in a low, somber voice.

"Dad, put on a tape!" Ethan repeated impatiently.

James saw that Christina and Terri were staring at the TV screen.

"Police believe that a hitchhiker beat Eckridge and then stole his car. Eckridge's wife told police that her sixty-eight-year-old husband traveled a lot for business and liked to pick up hitchhikers to keep him company. A statewide manhunt has begun to find the alleged — "

"A tape, Dad! A tape!" Ethan chanted. "I want cartoons!"

"Okay, okay," Paul shouted. He switched off the TV.

James saw Christina and Terri whispering to each other. Then they both turned to look at him, troubled expressions on their faces.

"Hey, how about a short walk?" James suggested. "You know. Get some air." He started to the front door. "Anyone want to join me?"

Still staring at him, the girls didn't reply. So he headed out the door by himself.

Chapter 8

Later, James tried to get comfortable on the living room couch. But it was exactly one inch too short for him to stretch out. And no matter which way he turned, one of the cushion zippers dug into his back.

He sat up, pushed away the cotton blanket Paula had given him, and let his eyes wander around the dark room. It was so hot. Like trying to sleep in a hot closet.

He began to get that suffocating feeling again. The same feeling he had felt right after dinner. That's why he had hurried out of the house. That's why he'd had to breathe some fresh air.

That feeling followed him, tightening his chest until he started to gasp for air. But getting out of the house had helped. Walking had helped.

Now, in the darkness, listening to the creaks and squeaks of the unfamiliar house, he fought back the feeling. One deep breath. Then another.

"Don't hurt me, James. Please — don't hurt me."

Shut up, shut up, shut UP! he thought, silently screaming the words in his mind.

"Please don't hurt me."

Shut up, shut up, SHUT UP!

He wiped his forehead with the end of the blanket. He realized he was bathed in sweat.

He was still fully dressed, except for his sneakers. Should he sneak outside for another walk?

Before he could decide, he heard the creak of the stairs.

Footsteps.

He tossed the blanket away. He climbed to his feet.

He took a deep breath. Another deep breath.

Someone was coming down the stairs. Whoever it was was trying not to be heard.

Shadows moved near the stairway. Someone slipped into the living room.

"James?" A whispered voice. "Are you awake?"

"Christina!" He took a step toward her. "Hi."

He could see her clearly now in the light through the living room window. She was wearing a long, white T-shirt that nearly covered her shorts. Her hair fell in tangles about her face.

"I couldn't sleep," she whispered.

They sat down together on the couch. She smelled lemony, James realized. He liked the smell.

She leaned close to him and smiled. "I guess I'm overtired or something."

"Maybe it's the heat," he whispered.

"Sometimes I get afraid in new places," she confessed in a little girl voice.

James wasn't sure he believed her. She didn't seem to be the type to be afraid — of anything. He put his arm around her shoulders. She didn't resist him.

She raised her face to his. Her lips found his.

Her lips were hot and dry. He pulled her closer. The suffocating feeling was gone.

She smelled so lemony. Her breath was warm on his face.

She moved her lips against his. The kiss lasted a long time.

"You're dangerous," she whispered breathily when they finally pulled apart. "You're really dangerous — aren't you, James."

"I'm going to ride with you girls to Cleveland, if that's okay," James said.

They were seated around the dining room table. Paula had insisted on serving them big stacks of pancakes "for the road" before they left.

Christina reacted to James's news with a pleased smile. It actually wasn't news to her. He had told her the night before.

The night before.

He closed his eyes.

He could still feel her warm face pressing against his, still feel the touch of her dry, insistent lips.

Terri didn't react at all. She glared for an instant at Christina, then lowered her eyes to her plate, still stacked high with pancakes drowning in syrup. "Are you going to chip in for gas?" she asked James coldly, deliberately not looking at him.

"Yeah. Sure," he told Terri. "No problem."

"I think you should stay here in Tampa," Paul said to James, wiping his chin with a paper napkin.

"What for?" James asked, pouring himself a glass of orange juice.

"Why not?" Paul replied. "What have you got going in Cleveland, of all places?"

James shrugged.

"We're putting up a new resort hotel," Paul said, "on the Seventeenth Street Causeway. You know. On the water. I could get you a job. No problem."

"A construction job?" James asked, stirring his fork around in the puddle of syrup on his empty plate.

"Yeah," Paul said, tossing down his napkin. "What's wrong with that? You too good for construction these days?"

"Thanks, anyway," James said quickly, raising a hand as if to fend off his cousin. He climbed to his feet. Christina and Terri followed his lead.

"We've got to go," James said. He gave his cousin a playful punch on the shoulder. "You've been terrific, Paul."

"Think about what I'm telling you," Paul insisted. "You could make some real money, man."

James waved him off.

They stopped in the kitchen to say good-bye to Paula. Then, carrying their bags, Christina and Terri made their way to the car.

James tracked down Ethan to say good-bye. "You going to remember me next time?" he asked.

Ethan thought about it. "Maybe," he replied seriously. "Will you bring me a present next time?"

"Yeah. Okay," James agreed. "Then you'll remember me?"

"Maybe."

James called good-bye to Paul and Paula again. Then, hoisting his canvas bag, he hurried out the front door.

He stopped on the front stoop. He could see that Christina and Terri were having an argument behind the car. Terri was waving her arms, gesturing angrily. Christina was half-sitting, half-leaning on the trunk, shaking her head.

They're arguing about me, James realized.

Well, too bad, Terri, he thought, watching them. I'm coming along.

Christina wants me to come with you, and so you lose.

He could feel his anger beginning to rise.

What was Terri's problem, anyway? He'd never done anything to her. Why didn't she like him?

He stepped off the stoop and made his way quickly to the driveway, taking long strides. They stopped arguing as soon as they saw him. Christina pulled open the trunk. They tossed their bags inside.

"Who's driving?" Terri asked, unable to completely erase the anger from her voice.

"I'll drive. I'm in the mood," James said.

Neither of them argued with him. He saw Terri cast another angry glance at Christina as she climbed into the back seat.

Maybe Terri is jealous, he thought. Yeah. Maybe

that's it. She's upset about Christina and me. She's jealous.

Smiling over that idea, he climbed behind the wheel.

He had started the engine and was about to back down the drive when he heard Paul calling from the house. "Stop! Whoa! Hold it!"

Through the windshield, James saw Paul leap off the front stoop and come running toward them. James lowered the window and called out. "Hey — what's wrong!"

"My wallet!" Paul cried angrily. "My wallet is missing!"

Chapter 9

Paul angrily jerked open the car door, his blue eyes bulging, his face bright red. "My wallet," he repeated. "Come on, man — where is it?"

"Now, hold on," James told him, turning out of the seat and lowering both feet to the ground. "Hold on, Paul — "

"Where is it?" Paul demanded, his face twisted in anger. "We're talking a thousand bucks here, man. This isn't one of your little candy store shopliftings."

"Hey!" James angrily leapt from the car. "That was a long time ago. Why are you bringing that up?"

"No discussions," Paul snapped. He reached out a hand. Then he spoke slowly, menacingly, lowering his voice. "Just give me the wallet."

James tried to back away from the outstretched hand, but Paul had him pinned against the car. "I don't have your wallet, man."

A wave of anger swept over James. He could feel every muscle in his body tighten.

Christina and Terri hadn't moved. They sat frozen in the car, staring out the windows, their expressions alarmed, frightened.

Paul stuck his upturned palm under James's nose. "The wallet, man. Just hand me the wallet."

The anger swarmed through James's body, pulsed at his temples. He cried out and shoved Paul's hand away. "Get your hand out of my face."

Paul's eyes narrowed. He didn't back up. "It was right on the shelf, James. Right by the door. You're not leaving till I get my wallet."

"You're always losing things, Paul," James said, stiffening his body, balling his hands into fists as if preparing for a fight. "You're always losing everything. You probably took it upstairs when you went to bed last night."

"The wallet," Paul insisted, ignoring James's words. Again, he stuck his open hand in James's face. "Just give me the wallet."

James roughly shoved the hand away. "I'm not a thief."

"The wallet. I want the wallet."

Christina's voice broke through their shouts. "Come on, James — we have to get going."

"You're not going anywhere," Paul insisted.

Paul grabbed James's shoulder.

The anger overtook James. Everything turned red.

He swung without warning. His fist caught Paul completely by surprise. Paul uttered a loud groan, his eyes ballooning as James's fist connected with his chin.

Paul's eyes fluttered, then rolled up in his head. Both arms flew up into the air as if he were going to take off. Then he collapsed in a heap beside the driveway.

"Paul, what's going on?" James heard Paula call from the house.

"Let's get moving," James said to Christina and Terri.

He dived into the driver's seat and threw the car into reverse before closing the door. He floored the gas pedal, and the car lurched backwards down the drive.

As he started to pull away, James saw Paula running across the lawn toward her fallen husband, her arms flailing out at her sides, her mouth open wide in distress. He could hear her screaming Paul's name over and over. And then her voice was drowned out by the car engine as James roared away.

He didn't even slow down until they were out of the development, heading along the service road back toward the highway.

No one spoke.

James was breathing so hard, he felt as if his chest were about to explode.

Terri was the one to break the heavy silence. "This isn't good," she muttered, sitting slumped in the back seat, her head down, away from the window as if she were hiding. "This isn't good, Christina."

"Shut up, Terri," Christina snapped. "Just shut up."

"I *won't!*" Terri insisted shrilly. "This isn't good. I'm telling you."

"Shut up, Terri. I mean it," Christina shouted. "Just shut up for once."

Terri uttered an angry, exasperated cry, but didn't say any more.

They drove past small, white houses. Cypress trees leaned over the road. An orange sun was climbing the sky to their right. It was already hot and sticky.

"You really hit him," Christina said quietly, playing with a strand of blonde hair.

"Lucky punch," James replied, keeping his eyes on the road. "Have you seen any signs for Route 75?"

"Up there." Christina pointed. "We're going the right way. Look at those palm trees. They're so tall."

James slowed for a stop sign.

"You been in a lot of fights?" Christina asked.

He shrugged. "A few." He was still waiting for his heart to stop thudding, for the blood to stop pulsing at his temples, for his hands to stop shaking.

Terri shifted noisily in the back seat. He heard her mutter something under her breath, but he couldn't make out the words.

"I'm not a thief," he said, his voice breaking. "How could he call me a thief?"

"He was just upset," Christina replied. She placed her hand on his shoulder, as if to calm him.

"I'm not a thief," James insisted. "He had no right to — to *do* that." He gripped the steering wheel tighter, trying to force his hands to stop trembling. "Did he really think I'd steal from my own cousin?"

Christina lowered her hand to his knee. "It *is* strange about the wallet," she said softly.

He glanced at her. "Huh? What do you mean?"

She thought for a moment before replying. "Well, the last time I noticed, the wallet *was* right by the front door. On that shelf with the keys and stuff."

"So?" James asked defensively.

"So nothing," she said curtly. "I just said it was strange, that's all."

He saw that she was staring at him, an accusing look on her face. She kept her eyes locked on him, as if waiting for him to confess.

Angrily, he stared straight ahead. He suddenly realized he was gritting his teeth so hard, his jaw hurt.

He lowered his foot on the gas pedal as the highway entrance came into view on the right, and the car shot forward. "Stop staring at me," he snapped.

"Okay. Fine." She turned away from him and stared out the passenger window. "I didn't say anything. You don't have to bite my head off."

"Hey, are we having fun yet?" Terri asked sarcastically from the back seat.

"Shut up, Terri," Christina snarled. "I'm warning you . . ."

James maneuvered the car onto the highway and moved into the center lane. The speedometer told him he was doing seventy-five.

Christina continued to stare out the side window.

James snapped on the radio. It came on too loud. Music roared from the speakers, startling all three of them. He turned down the volume and began pushing buttons, moving quickly from station to station.

"Watch the road," Terri warned shrilly. "You'll get us all killed."

He ignored her and continued pushing buttons. He stopped at a Guns 'n' Roses song he recognized.

"Ugh. Axl Rose," Terri muttered disgustedly.

The song ended and was followed by a long Metallica cut. "I like this station," James said to no one in particular.

"I knew you'd be a metal moron," Terri said nastily.

"Guess you're still into New Kids on the Block, right?" he shot back sarcastically.

She didn't reply.

They drove on for a while, the whining guitars of the heavy metal music drowning out all other sounds. No one talked.

A little before noon, the news came on. James reached to change the station, but Christina pushed his hand away.

A smooth-voiced woman gave the weather forecast, then read the news: "Roger Eckridge, the elderly Fort Lauderdale man beaten and robbed allegedly by a hitchhiker, died of his injuries this morning at Fort Lauderdale General. Police are intensifying their efforts — "

James switched off the radio.

"Why can't they just play music?" he grumbled.

"If I wanted news, I'd buy a paper."

To his surprise, Christina was glaring at him, her eyes wide, her expression thoughtful. She tugged nervously at her hair, twisting and untwisting one of her corkscrew curls around one finger.

"Hey, let's lighten up, okay?" James pleaded. "Why are you looking at me like that?"

"Pull over," Terri's voice, loud and frightened, rang out from the back seat.

"Huh?" James cried.

"Pull over," Terri insisted sternly. "Right now. Christina and I have got to talk."

Chapter 10

"Hey, what's the problem?" James asked, edging into the right lane.

"It's between Christina and me," Terri replied coldly.

James looked questioningly at Christina, who was staring back at him, a troubled expression on her face. "Just pull over," she said.

James obediently slowed the car and rolled onto the grassy shoulder. As soon as the car stopped, both girls pushed their doors open and stepped out. A blast of hot, wet air entered the car before they slammed the doors.

Resting his head against the leather headrest, James watched them walk away from the car along the shoulder. Cars whirred by. A two-sectioned oil truck rumbled past.

Several yards from the car, the girls stopped and confronted each other. James squinted into the sunlight, studying them as they argued.

Terri seemed very frightened, very upset.

Christina seemed angry.

Terri's face grew red as she shouted, gesturing with her hands and pacing back and forth along the side of the highway in front of Christina. Christina had her hands on her hips and kept shaking her head. Terri was doing almost all of the talking.

Girls, girls, thought James, you shouldn't fight over me.

Really. There's enough of me to go around.

He snickered to himself, then cut it short when he realized that Terri was crying.

What is she so upset about? he wondered, leaning forward, resting his arms on top of the steering wheel as he stared at them through the windshield. Why does Terri seem so scared?

Christina started to comfort Terri, but Terri pulled away from her, and the argument started again. Both girls kept glancing back at James.

They're definitely talking about me, he decided.

I guess Terri is real scared of me for some reason. And Christina is telling her to lighten up and give me a break.

He was tempted to get out of the car, go over, and break up the dispute. He reached for the door handle, then decided to wait a bit more.

He suddenly realized that his hand hurt. Holding it up in front of him, he saw that the knuckles along the back had been cut and were caked with dried blood.

I guess I *did* hit Paul pretty hard, he decided, rubbing the hand gently. I hit him hard enough to cut my hand open.

What a shame, he thought. What a shame.

The visit had ended so badly.

Like a lot of other visits.

He had hoped to get away cleanly this time. But no such luck.

What a shame. What a shame, he repeated to himself.

But at least I got a little spending money out of it.

He rubbed his eyes. They felt dry and irritated. Probably just from staring into the glare of the sun.

When he opened them, the two girls were still arguing.

Maybe I should just get out and walk away, he thought. I'm causing all this trouble. All this discussion. Who needs it?

"Please don't hurt me, James. Please."

Yeah. He and Melissa had had enough discussions, enough arguments to last a lifetime. Enough arguments to send him on the run.

"Please don't hurt me." Every time he closed his eyes, he heard Melissa's pitiful plea, saw her dark eyes fill with fear.

Enough arguing, he thought, watching Christina and Terri through the Honda windshield.

I'll just wave good-bye and good riddance to them and hitch a ride by myself. To anywhere.

But then he had a better idea.

Why should he have to hitch? He had a car.

The keys were in the ignition. The engine was running. He was behind the wheel.

All he had to do was drive away.

The thought made him laugh out loud. What a hoot!

He *had* to do it. Just to see the looks on their faces as he bombed away.

Awesome! he thought. Truly awesome!

He peered out the windshield at them. Christina was doing the talking now, hands still on her hips, her blonde hair catching the light of the midday sun. Terri had her head lowered, her hands balled into tight fists at her sides, and was kicking at the tall grass.

Chuckling to himself, James reached for the gearshift and pulled it into drive. He checked the rearview mirror, then stepped on the gas.

He turned to see their mouths drop open in horror as he drove away.

Chapter 11

"James!" Christina screamed.

"What is he *doing*?" Terri cried. "Is he really driving away?"

The car rolled past them and kept going, keeping along the shoulder.

"Hey — James!"

Both girls started to run after it, shouting and waving their arms.

"He can't do this!" Terri yelled. "He *can't*!"

The car stopped about a hundred yards away, pulling back onto the grass. The girls kept running, frantically calling to James.

Gasping for breath, they pulled open the car doors and leaned into the car.

James was laughing uproariously, tossing back his head, slapping the steering wheel with both hands, enjoying his little joke.

"You're not funny," Christina said, still breathing hard.

"You should've seen the looks on your faces!"

James exclaimed through his convulsions of laughter.

"Why'd you do it?" Terri demanded angrily. She held her side, trying to rub away a cramp from running so hard.

"Just wanted to get your attention," James told her.

"You got it," Christina said breathlessly. "Don't do that again, okay?"

"Did I scare you?" James asked, very pleased with himself.

Christina didn't reply. She climbed into the front passenger seat. "We've got to get going," she said nervously, glancing at the passing cars on the highway. "Where are we, anyway?"

"We just passed Gainesvile, remember?" James said.

"We're still in Florida?"

"Yeah. Believe it or not," James replied. "We might make it to Georgia if you two — "

"I want to drive," Terri interrupted. She hurried around to the other side of the car and pulled open James's door.

He grinned up at her. "What's the matter? You don't trust me anymore?"

I *never* trusted you, Terri thought.

I never trusted you. And I never wanted to pick you up.

That was one of Christina's wonderful ideas, she thought bitterly. Just one of Christina's many wonderful ideas.

I wish we'd never stopped for you. I wish we'd never seen you. I wish —

"Okay. Give me a little room so I can get out," James broke into her unhappy thoughts.

Maybe I'm being unfair to him, Terri thought, stepping back and watching James climb out from behind the wheel.

Christina says I'm being unfair.

But why do we need him?

Terri had been so happy that they were dropping James off in Tampa. But now here he was, hanging on all the way to Cleveland.

And then what?

Would they be able to get rid of him then? Or would he follow them home? Move into one of their houses? Never go away?

I've got to stop these crazy thoughts, Terri warned herself.

But how *can* I? Everything is so . . . crazy.

If only James weren't so scary, she decided. If only he was someone we could trust.

But everything about him is so frightening. His size. His attitude. His terrible temper.

And what with the story on the radio about the old man . . .

"Terri, are you getting in or what?" Christina called impatiently.

"Sorry," Terri said softly, her mind still spinning. She turned her eyes to James, who was about to climb into the back seat, and felt a cold chill as she saw him staring back at her with the strangest smile on his face.

Then, instead of climbing in, Terri saw him tap on Christina's window. "Why don't you get in back with me?" he called.

"Huh? What did you say?" Christina rolled down her window.

"Come in back with me. We'll pretend we're in a big limo and Terri is our driver."

"Thanks a bunch," Terri said dryly, rolling her eyes.

"Come on," James urged Christina. He pulled open her door and tugged her arm, flashing her an inviting smile.

I don't believe this, Terri thought unhappily. They're going to make out while I drive the car.

Christina is too much! Terri thought, feeling angry and jealous at the same time. How can she do this?

Easy, Terri decided.

She climbed behind the wheel with a loud sigh, and pulled the car door closed.

Christina piled into the back seat and James immediately pulled her onto his lap. She squealed. "Let go!"

James laughed and raised his arms, freeing her to scoot onto the seat.

"We're never getting out of here," Terri moaned.

"Just drive," Christina instructed, giggling because James was tickling her.

"I don't believe you two," Terri complained, pulling onto the highway.

"You're welcome to join us," James told her, grinning.

"Don't be disgusting," Terri quickly replied.

"Yeah. Don't be disgusting," Christina teased.

Terri clicked on the radio, turning up the volume so she wouldn't have to listen to the other two. She kept the car in the center lane, cruising at a steady sixty.

As she drove, she tried to clear her mind, letting the music roll over her thoughts, letting the music push out everything she didn't want to think about, concentrating on it, flowing with it as if the music were driving the car, carrying her forward, carrying her away, away from Florida, away from Christina, away from James, the hitchhiker.

The hitchhiker. The hitchhiker.

The word played over and over in her mind, repeating itself until it seemed to have no meaning.

Every once in a while, she would raise her eyes to the rearview mirror and see Christina and James wrapped up in each other, kissing passionately.

Then she would quickly turn her eyes back to the highway and let the music carry her away.

"Hope you two are nice and cozy back there," Terri called back to them sarcastically.

Christina mumbled a reply. Terri couldn't hear it over the music.

This isn't the first time Christina has done this, she thought.

It isn't the first time Christina has had a guy and I haven't.

But why now? And why with some scary guy we don't know a thing about?

A hitchhiker. Hitchhiker. Hitchhiker.

It's just too dangerous, Terri thought. If only I could convince her.

She thought of the story on the radio. The old man who died.

Hitchhiker. Hitchhiker. Hitchhiker.

She had tried reasoning with Christina. When that hadn't worked, she had tried tears.

What did she have to do?

What *could* she do?

There they were, going at it hot and heavy in the back seat while she drove them like some kind of chauffeur.

Don't let yourself get mad, Terri. Just get into the music. Into the music. Let the music carry you away, as it has so many times before when you were stressed out.

The melody of an old Rolling Stones record floated into Terri's head, a song her parents liked to play again and again. . . .

"Hitchhike . . . hitchhike, baby. Hitchhike . . ."

They stopped for chili dogs at a stand just over the Georgia border. Then Terri drove the rest of the afternoon with only a five-minute rest stop to stretch their legs.

As evening arrived, the sun slowly lowered itself behind an endless row of pine trees on their left. The sky was pink, the color of bubble gum, lighter than the pink clay along the shoulder of the highway.

The road had narrowed to two lanes here. There were few cars on the highway, mostly large trucks roaring along at about eighty.

"Hey — anybody getting hungry?" Christina called from the back seat.

"Any place to stop around here?" James asked, beside her. He'd been napping, and his voice was hoarse from sleep.

"We have to get a map, you know?" Christina said. She shook James, trying to rouse him. "Wake up, you bum."

"Are we going to stop?" James asked sleepily. "I'm starving. Where are we, anyway?"

"Hey, Terri, what's the matter?" Christina asked, her voice suddenly filling with concern. "You're not saying anything."

"Uh, guys . . ." Terri said reluctantly, her eyes raised to the rearview mirror. "I have some bad news. I think we're being followed."

Chapter 12

"Huh?"

Christina and James both uttered their surprise.

Terri accelerated to pass a small pickup truck loaded with a mound of white sand.

"How do you know?" Christina asked, her voice tight with fear. She twisted around to gaze out the back window.

"That blue car has been behind us since Gainesville," Terri said, pressing down further on the gas pedal. The car hesitated, then roared forward. The speedometer read eighty-five.

"I don't see any blue car," James said. He, too, had turned to peer out the back.

"Just watch," Terri said, her voice calm, despite the frightened fluttering in her chest.

A few seconds later, a blue Taurus passed the pickup truck and moved back into the lane, several car lengths behind them.

"That's the blue car?" Christina asked.

"That's it," Terri said, watching it in the rearview mirror.

The sun sank lower behind the trees. Lengthening shadows cast the highway in black and gray.

"Well, what makes you think it's following us?" Christina asked shrilly.

"Yeah," James added, "maybe it's just heading north like we are."

"I don't think so," Terri said. "I've been watching it for a long time. It always stays in the same lane I'm in. It keeps pretty far back, but not *that* far back. Sometimes I slowed down to let it pass me — but it slowed down, too. It wouldn't pass."

Christina and James stared back at the blue Taurus. "I can't see the driver very well," Christina said. "It's getting too dark."

"It's a man. That's all I know," Terri reported. "He hasn't gotten close enough for me to see his face."

She eased her foot on the brake and slowed the car to fifty. Several car lengths behind them, the blue car slowed, too, keeping the same distance between them.

"See what I mean?" Terri asked, suddenly sounding very frightened. "Hey, you two — turn around. What if he knows *we* know he's following us?"

"But why would anyone follow us?" Christina asked, settling back into her seat, then slumping low.

"I still don't believe — " James started.

"Oh, I know!" Christina interrupted. "It's Paul."

"Huh?" James cried.

"I'll bet it's your cousin, Paul. He's coming after us for his money."

"Hey!" James shouted angrily. "What makes you think I've got it? I told you — "

"There's an exit," Terri interrupted. "I'm taking it. Hold on!"

She spun the wheel. The tires squealed as the car swerved onto the exit ramp.

Terri accelerated, struggling to follow the sharp curve of the exit road, sliding on the narrow gravel shoulder, the tires spinning noisily. Regaining the road, she floored the gas pedal. The car shot forward onto a narrow, unpaved road.

"Look out!"

The slow-moving tractor appeared from out of nowhere, crossing the road just up ahead of them. The driver was looking the other way.

Christina screamed.

Terri spun the wheel. The car slid off the road, bounced onto the grass, bumped over some rocks, the engine roaring.

A tree trunk whirred past the window, leaves and branches brushing the car noisily.

The tractor was behind them now. Terri spun the wheel back toward the road.

The car bounced hard. Terri's head struck the roof.

She spun the wheel again, her foot on the brake.

And then they were back on the road with a jolt, the tires squealing, then catching hard, and the car spurting forward as if shot from a cannon.

"I don't believe it!" Christina gasped. She was tugging at the sides of her hair with both hands.

In the mirror, Terri could see James holding onto

her. James looked pale and shaken, even in the flickering, shadowy light. "Did we lose the blue Taurus?" he asked.

Terri glanced through the rearview mirror. "Yes, it's gone," she said with a relieved sigh. And then her expression darkened as she continued to watch the mirror. "No. Here he comes. He's still there."

"We've got to lose him!" Christina cried. "Turn here!"

Terri obediently spun the wheel sharply, and the car squealed onto another narrow country road. A few seconds later, they could hear another squeal of tires behind them as the Taurus made the turn.

"He's picking up speed," Terri reported. She swallowed hard. "I think he's trying to catch us now."

The Honda bumped over the country road. Christina and James held onto each other as Terri floored the gas pedal. The engine whined, and the car responded with a burst of speed.

"He's catching up!" Terri cried, her voice revealing her fear.

"Who *is* he?" Christina demanded. "What does he *want*?"

The car dipped into a hole in the road. Terri hit the brake. Too late. All three passengers cried out as their heads hit the roof with a jolt.

The road curved to the right. Terri steadied herself, her head throbbing, and struggled to follow the road, glancing at the blue Taurus in the mirror as it roared closer.

"Hey — the highway!" she exclaimed.

"We must've made a circle," James said quietly.

Terri edged the car onto the highway, then swerved into the center lane.

"We can't lose him on this road," Christina said. "He'll just follow us forever."

"Look for a town," James urged. "We'll be safer in a town."

"If only there were more cars on this road," Terri complained. "We could lose him — "

"Oh!"

None of them realized that the blue Taurus had caught up with them until it pulled alongside in the left lane, then swerved to bump them.

"Hey!"

The car bumped the driver's side again, tossing the Honda like a carnival bumper-car ride.

"He's trying to push us off the road!" James cried.

"He's trying to *kill* us!" Christina exclaimed.

Another hard bump. Metal against metal at sixty miles an hour.

What do I do? Terri thought, feeling the panic run through her body.

What do I do? What do I do? What do I do?

Got to think clearly. Got to think . . .

But the fear swept over her, paralyzed her, made her mind go blank.

The Taurus slammed into their side again. Harder this time.

"He's *crazy*!" Terri screamed.

Trying to fight down the panic, she hit the brake. The Honda went into a slide, screeching into the right lane — and then onto the gravel shoulder.

"Terri — *no!*"

She heard Christina's shrill scream from the back seat.

And then the crunch of metal and glass.

Terri was thrown forward. Then tossed back. She felt her seatbelt catch at her waist, hold her in as her head started to throb.

The car had come to a stop, she realized.

Am I alive?

The question floated past her.

She seemed to be swimming in the shadows. Everything was moving and not moving. The car was floating, bobbing around in dark waters. Or was it just in her mind?

A hand touched her shoulder.

"Are you okay? Terri?" Christina's voice.

The shadows lifted.

"We hit a tree." James voice, high-pitched, un-certain.

The words seemed to clear her mind.

"We hit a tree."

Terri blinked. Once. Twice. She moved her head around, testing her neck muscles. "I — I'm okay," she stammered uncertainly.

She peered out through the windshield. The car was tilted up at a low angle. The right headlight beamed through the darkness, illuminating a clump of evergreens. The left headlight appeared to be out.

"We're okay," Christina said, her voice strangely muffled. "We're all okay."

"Look." Terri pointed to the road.

The blue Taurus had stopped several yards up ahead. Now it was slowly backing up toward them.

"Can we move? He's coming! We've got to move!" Christina urged, squeezing Terri's shoulder.

"I — I don't know," Terri replied, her voice a frightened whisper.

She threw the car into reverse and stepped hard on the gas.

Silence.

She hadn't realized that the engine had cut off.

A moment of panic.

Then she fumbled for the key. Turned it.

The engine whined. But didn't start.

"Try again! Quick!" Christina cried.

The blue Taurus was backing up, just a few yards up ahead now.

Terri tried the key again, pumping hard on the gas. The car made a grinding protest.

"I think you flooded it," James said.

The blue Taurus came to a stop at the edge of the highway. The driver's door opened. The car light came on. They could see a man wearing dark clothes climbing out of the car.

"We're trapped," Terri said softly. "He's got us."

Chapter 13

"Who is it?" Christina asked in a whisper. "I can't see his face!"

James grabbed the door handle and pushed open the back door. "Come on — into the woods!" He grabbed Christina's hand and tugged.

Christina hesitated, her eyes locked on the dark figure climbing out of the car.

"We're trapped," Terri repeated, gripping the steering wheel with both hands, making no attempt to escape from the Honda.

"Come *on!* Hurry!" James frantically urged, stepping out onto the dirt.

Terri reached for the door handle, but made no move to pull it.

"Terri?" Christina called. "Do you think — ?"

She stopped as a set of yellow blinking lights came into view on the road.

The lights seemed to float low above the ground, blinking steadily like twinkling stars, growing larger and brighter as they approached.

Frozen in place, Terri turned her attention to the

blinking lights as they moved along the highway, then appeared to float toward her.

"Hey — it's a tow truck!" James called excitedly from just outside the car. "Hey!" He waved both arms above his head, signalling the approaching truck.

The blinking lights glowed brighter. Terri squinted, and the truck came into focus beneath them. Its tires crunched over the gravel highway shoulder and rolled onto the dirt.

"You all right in there?" a voice called from the cab. A head poked out of the tow truck window. The man had a cigar in his mouth. He was wearing a red baseball cap. "You kids okay?"

"Yeah. We're not hurt." James walked around the back of the car, his hands jammed into his jeans pockets, and approached the tow truck.

"Smashed up your headlight." The door swung open, and the truck driver hopped down.

Terri saw that he was tall and lean, with scraggly dark hair down to his shoulders. He tossed the cigar to the ground. He walked over to the driver's door and peered in at Terri. "How'd it happen?"

"We were being chased," Terri blurted out. "That car was chasing us, and — " She started to point to the man in the blue Taurus.

But the man and the car were gone.

The truck driver turned to follow the direction of her finger. "Huh?"

"He must have driven away," James explained.

"I don't believe it," Christina muttered from the back seat.

Terri exhaled loudly. She felt shaken, but relieved.

The tow truck driver narrowed his eyes suspiciously. "You kids on something? You been drinking?"

"No," James replied sharply, angered by the man's suspicion. "We just had an accident. That's all."

"Doesn't look too bad," the man said, removing his cap, scratching his greasy hair, then replacing the cap. "Will it start?"

"I don't think so," Terri replied.

"Let me give it a try, okay?" He pulled open the door and helped Terri out.

She stood shakily, but quickly caught her balance. She turned her eyes to the highway, to the spot where the blue Taurus had parked. Nothing there now. Gone. Whoever it was must have driven off as soon as he saw the blinking lights of the tow truck.

Whoever it was. Terri sucked in a deep breath of the cool air, starting to feel a little better.

Christina climbed out and joined the other two. They stood in a line, watching the tow truck operator lower himself into the front seat, folding his long legs into the car.

He turned the key in the ignition, and the car started right up. Then he slowly backed up, moving the car off the tree trunk. As the car inched backwards, Terri could see that the damage wasn't too bad. The left headlight was shattered. The bumper was bent in, but not enough to interfere with the tire.

"They put good bumpers on these cars. You don't even need a tow." The man climbed out of the car. "You kids were lucky."

"Yeah. Lucky," Christina muttered, casting a dark glance at Terri.

"Better get the headlight replaced. There's a garage in town that might still be open."

"Town? Where's town?" Terri asked eagerly.

The driver pointed. "Next right." He raised his hand to the brim of his cap as if to tip it. "Drive carefully." He started back to his truck, taking long strides.

"Thanks," James called after him.

"And I'd watch out for those car chases with invisible cars," the man said, and he disappeared into his truck.

The motel room was sparse, but clean. James tossed his canvas bag on the armchair in the corner, and flopped onto his back on the bed.

Sleepy's. That was the name of the long, two-story motel at the far end of the small town.

The service garage had been closed. James and the girls were too tired and shaken to keep driving. And Terri was afraid they'd be stopped by the police for having only one headlight.

So they had stopped at Sleepy's for the night, parking the car in the back of the motel where it would be hidden from the street, hidden from the man in the blue Taurus in case he was still looking for them.

James stared up at the shadows playing across the low ceiling. A brass sprinkler was positioned right over the bed. The room smelled of disinfectant. The air conditioner under the window rattled.

Closing his eyes, he heard voices in the next room. Christina's voice. Terri's voice. Shrill and angry.

They were having another loud argument.

What's it about this time? he wondered, keeping his eyes shut, listening hard.

The wall muffled their words.

Didn't we have enough excitement for one day? What could they possibly be fighting about?

He thought about Christina. She's so hot, he told himself. She's a real babe. We should go back to Key West and *really* party!

Thinking about Key West pulled Melissa into his mind. He saw her again, her face red and puffy, her coppery hair tangled and damp, tear tracks staining her pale cheeks. And for the thousandth time he saw her tiny, clenched fists, and heard her desperate plea to him not to hurt her.

With a pained sigh, he rolled onto his side and buried his face in the bedspread. The woolen bedspread felt scratchy against his skin. He heard water running in the room above his. A toilet flushed.

He raised his arm over his head, covering his exposed ear, trying to shut out Christina's and Terri's voices from next door. They were still going at it. He could hear Terri shouting, even with his ears covered.

"What is your *problem*?" he asked aloud.

He thought about the car. They could probably drive all the way to Cleveland without getting it fixed. Of course, driving at night would be risky. . . .

The shouting from next door stopped suddenly. James uncovered his ear and raised his head, listening intently.

Yes. They had finally stopped.

Had Terri won? he wondered. Had she persuaded Christina to dump him? To leave him here and go on their way without him?

Is that what they were arguing about?

He felt a hot stab of anger start in his stomach.

Terri had no reason to get on his case. Just because she was jealous. . . .

The anger started to spread.

You'd better not mess with me, Terri, he thought.

You've picked the wrong guy to mess with.

James's thoughts were interrupted by a loud knock on the door.

Startled, he sat up with a jerk.

The loud knock was repeated. Someone banging hard on the wooden door.

James quickly climbed to his feet and made his way across the room.

He had his hand on the knob when a husky voice called in: "Come out with your hands up!"

Chapter 14

James froze with his hand on the doorknob. His breath caught in his throat.

He put his ear to the door and listened. But all he could hear was the pounding of his heart.

Then he heard a soft giggle.

He turned the knob and jerked open the door.

"Terri!"

Her blue eyes caught the light of the dim hallway ceiling light. "Gotcha," she said, and burst out laughing. She had changed into denim cutoffs and a pink midriff top.

James gaped at her, waiting for his heart to stop thudding. "Hey, that wasn't funny," he snapped. "I — I didn't recognize your voice."

He realized it was the first time he'd seen her laugh.

"The look on your face as you opened the door," she said, shaking her head. "Priceless."

"Glad you enjoyed it," he replied sarcastically. He had a sudden urge to punch her, to wipe the grin off her face. But he forced the thought from his mind. "What's going on?"

Her face turned serious. She pushed a strand of black hair off her forehead. "I just thought maybe we could talk," she said reluctantly, avoiding his eyes. She fumbled for words. "I mean, I sort of wanted to apologize."

"Huh?" He couldn't hide his surprise.

He was standing awkwardly in the doorway, still holding onto the doorknob. A fly buzzed noisily against the hallway light. The hallway smelled of stale cigarette smoke. "Want to come in?" he asked, taking a step back.

"Could we . . . uh . . . take a walk? She raised her eyes to his and gave him a shy smile.

His mind was spinning. Why was she doing this? What did she want? Where was Christina?

What was going on?

"Don't look at me like that," she said playfully. "I'm not going to kidnap you. I just thought we might take a walk so I could apologize for being so awful to you."

"Yeah. Sure. Okay," he replied uncertainly, scratching his jaw.

Leaving the door open, he turned and walked to the dresser to pick up his wallet and room key. "I could use some fresh air," he called back to her. "This air conditioner is just a noise machine."

"In our room, too," Terri said.

A short while later, they were walking side by side across the parking lot in front of the motel. The air was cool and dry. The inky sky was clear and dotted with bright stars. The pink and green neon Sleepy's sign reflected off their clothes, making them change colors as they walked.

They stopped at the edge of the parking lot. The small town with its low, two-story shops angled down a gently sloping hill to the right. To their left, a flat field led to a dark pine forest.

James hesitated. Terri took his arm and led him in the direction of the trees. "Nice out," she said shyly, not letting go of his arm.

"Yeah," he agreed. "Where's Christina?" he blurted out.

A hurt expression crossed Terri's face for a brief moment. "She was tired. She wanted to try to sleep. But I'm too pumped to sleep. I mean, all that wild driving. I feel like I'm still in the car, still pushing down on the gas pedal, still trying to get away from that — from whoever it was chasing after us."

"What a day," he muttered.

"Besides, I didn't want Christina to come," Terri said. A sly smile curled her lips. She squeezed his arm. "I wanted you all to myself for once."

What's going on here? James wondered, keeping his eyes on the dark trees up ahead. Is Terri coming on to me? I thought she hated my guts.

The field was soft and marshy. A heavy dew had made the tall grass wet. Cicadas chirped out a loud, shrill symphony.

"What were you two fighting about?" James asked.

"You heard us?" Terri looked up at him in surprise. She lost her footing for a second, her sneaker slipping on the marshy ground. James held onto her arm and she regained her balance. "I guess the walls are pretty thin, huh?"

He nodded.

"Well, we were just letting off steam," she said, staring ahead at the trees looming over them, black shadows against the star-filled sky. "It wasn't really about anything."

"I see," James said, not believing a word of it.

"You know, sometimes all the tension just gets to you," she continued. "And you just have to shout a bit, get it out of your system."

"Sounded like a pretty good fight," James insisted.

They were under the trees now, their sneakers crunching softly over a thick carpet of pine needles. They both took a deep breath. The air smelled piney and sweet.

"It wasn't a real fight," Terri told him. "Christina and I have been friends for a long time. We know each other so well. We know we can yell and carry on and get all our feelings out, and the other person won't take it the wrong way."

"I see," James replied, trying to sound as if he believed her. He didn't. Christina and Terri had disagreed about *something*. That he knew. Most likely, they had disagreed about him.

But now here he was, walking in these dark woods with Terri, asking her questions and getting lies in return.

What did she really want?

Suddenly, he heard a cracking sound. The sound

of a twig breaking under someone's foot.

They both stopped. Terri had heard it, too. Her eyes widened in fear. She gripped his arm as they listened.

Another cracking sound. Rustling. Nearby.

Terri leaned against him. He could feel her body trembling.

Another cracking sound. A footstep.

Closer.

"We're not alone," James whispered.

Chapter 15

Shards of pale moonlight filtered down through the thick trees. Long shadows stretched across the ground, like dark holes. There was no breeze, no wind at all.

James and Terri stood in place, listening to the soft rustlings, the muffled sound of footsteps over the covering of dried pine needles.

"Who — who's there?" Terri finally managed to cry.

No reply.

"Is anybody there?" Terri repeated, casting a frightened glance at James.

Again, no reply.

Another footstep.

"Look!" James pointed down to the ground.

Terri turned to follow his gaze, and saw the two intruders scurrying across the path. "Possums," she said.

"Yeah. Possums."

Still holding onto each other, they both burst out laughing.

"I knew it was some kind of animal all along," James said, starting to walk again, pushing a clump of tall weeds out of the way.

"Yeah. Right," Terri replied skeptically.

"You sure scare easy," he teased.

"I didn't get scared until I saw how scared *you* were," she shot back.

He laughed and turned back to her.

She caught up with him. Then, suddenly, she reached a hand up to his shoulder, tugged him down, and kissed him.

Her lips were warm and wet.

The kiss was short. After a few seconds, she pulled away and took a step back, her face expressionless. Her blue eyes searched his.

"What was that for?" he asked, unable to hide his surprise.

"That was my apology," she told him.

"Apology?"

"I told you. That's why I wanted to talk to you. I've been so mean to you. I just wanted to — "

Impulsively, he grabbed for her waist, tried to pull her to him to kiss her again.

But she backed out of his grasp.

"No."

He reached for her again. "Hey, what's the problem? Come here."

"No." She shook her head and stared at him. "That's not what I want. I just wanted to apologize. That's all."

"You're not a tease or anything, are you?" he asked, challenging her. His feelings were all mixed up now. He felt confused, angry, eager to kiss her again.

"James — just *listen* to me," she insisted shrilly. "I thought we might take a nice walk so I could apologize and we could be friends. I wasn't coming on to you. Really. I wouldn't do that to Christina."

"How will Christina know?" he asked, flashing her a devilish grin.

"Oh, don't be a pig," she shot back. "I told you. Christina and I have been friends forever. I'm not going to mess around with a boy she's interested in."

James pursed his lips in an exaggerated pout. "Shucks," he said sarcastically.

"Let's go back," Terri said wearily, her features drawn in disappointment. "I guess this was a bad idea."

She started to turn away from him, back toward the motel. But he grabbed her shoulders and spun her around.

"Get off! What are you doing?" she cried angrily, her blue eyes flaring.

James grinned at her teasingly. "I'm a big bad guy, Terri," he said. "Aren't you afraid to be all alone in these dark woods with me?"

She shook her head, but he saw a glint of fear in her eyes.

"Aren't you afraid?" he asked again.

He was awakened by pounding on the door to his room.

He raised his head and tried to blink himself

awake. Morning sunlight filtered through the window. He had been sleeping on his stomach, on top of his left arm. The arm tingled, numb.

Yawning, he pulled himself up. He grabbed the arm with his right hand and shook it, trying to wake it up.

The loud pounding on the door startled him again.

"Hey, James — wake up!" Christina's voice.

He squinted at the clock on the bedtable. Seven-fifteen.

Why so early? he thought. The circulation was beginning to return to the arm. He let it drop to his side.

"James — wake up!"

"I'm up," he called back.

"Open the door!" Christina called.

"Hold on." He climbed to his feet and stretched. He had slept in his underwear. Yawning again, he made his way to the armchair where he had tossed his jeans and pulled them on. Pine needles clung to the cuffs, he saw.

"James, open the door!" Christina called impatiently.

"Hold your horses," he said.

Starting to feel awake, he made his way to the door, undid the chain, and pulled it open.

Christina greeted him with a worried expression. "Is Terri in there with you?"

"Huh?" He squinted at her as if it would help him understand what she was asking.

"You heard me," she replied sharply. "Is Terri

in there with you?" She looked over his shoulder, trying to see into the room.

"No," he told her, backing up so she had a better view. "No way."

"Then where *is* she?" Christina asked, panic entering her voice.

James brushed back his hair with his hand. "What do you mean? She isn't with you?"

Christina shook her head. He saw her chin tremble. "She's gone."

"Are you sure?"

"Yes. She's gone. Oh, James — I'm so frightened. Terri's *disappeared!*"

Chapter 16

"Are you sure?" James stared at her in disbelief.

Christina pushed past him into the room. "Of *course* I'm sure." Her eyes scanned the room, as if she didn't believe him.

"Maybe she got up early and went out to get breakfast," James suggested.

Standing by the window, Christina shook her head. "I'm a very light sleeper. I would've heard her get up." She raised the shade and peered out into the sunlight. "Besides, her bed wasn't slept in."

James stepped into the center of the room, his mind whirring. He caught a glimpse of himself in the mirror over the dresser and realized that his hair was matted down from sleep, one side standing straight out.

"I heard you two going at it last night," he said, pulling his hairbrush from the canvas bag.

"So?" Christina asked defensively. She crossed her arms over her chest and tossed her hair back over her shoulder with a jerk of her head, a defiant gesture.

"Well, maybe Terri was angry at you and decided to split," James suggested, turning from the mirror to face her.

"No way," Christina replied, eyeing him coldly.

"What were you two arguing about, anyway?" he asked, turning back to the mirror and carefully brushing his hair.

He could see her in the corner of the mirror. She shrugged, as if to say it was nothing important, but her cheeks turned red. "It was no big deal," she told his reflection in the mirror. "It doesn't concern you."

He finished with his hair and tossed the brush into the canvas bag. Christina walked over to him and put her head on his chest. "Oh, James, I'm so scared. What do you think happened to her?"

Reflexively, he wrapped his arms around her shoulders and comforted her. "I still think she just split," he said softly.

"You're wrong,' she said, her face pressed against his chest. "I know Terri. She would've said something. She always had to have the last word. If she ditched us because she was angry, she'd have to tell me first."

Christina stifled a sob. James could feel her shoulders begin to tremble. He held her tighter.

"Besides," she said, her voice cracking, "her bag is still in the room. Unopened. She wouldn't go off without her bag."

James thought about it for a long moment. He was trying to decide whether or not to tell Christina he had been with Terri the night before. But his mind wasn't fully awake. He couldn't think clearly. He could never think clearly before breakfast.

"Maybe we should call the police," he said.

She pulled out of his arms, her face drawn in a tight frown. "Police? Do you think this tiny town even *has* police?"

James shrugged. "We could call and see."

"It would be a waste of time," Christina said, her dark eyes locked on his. "If there *is* a policeman or two in this disgusting place, how bright could they be? They probably spend their time pulling cats out of trees. They'd ask us hours of questions, and they wouldn't have a clue about how to find Terri."

James plopped down on the edge of the unmade bed. "Yeah. You're probably right," he reluctantly agreed. "Maybe you should call her parents. Up in Cleveland. Maybe Terri called them to tell them she was coming home or something."

"Her parents?" Christina uttered a hollow laugh. "They're the *last* people Terri would call."

"She and her parents don't get along?"

"They hardly speak. Terri had to sneak out of the house to come to Florida with me."

"Then maybe we should just wait for her to come back," James suggested.

Christina scowled. "Oh, sure. Brilliant idea." She shook her head unhappily and brushed some blonde curls off her face. "What if something has happened to her, James? What if she's lying hurt somewhere? Or — or — " Her voice caught in her throat. "Or worse? Don't forget, we were being followed yesterday. Somebody — "

"Okay, okay," James interrupted impatiently. "So we can't wait for her."

"Don't snap at me," Christina warned edgily.

He climbed to his feet. "I didn't snap at you. I — I'm just trying to think of what we should do."

"Let's drive around," Christina said thoughtfully. "Let's check out of this dump. Then drive around town. Drive around the whole area and see if we can find her."

"Okay." James reached over to the canvas bag and began to zip it up. "Sounds good." He smiled reassuringly at Christina. "Maybe we'll find her window shopping in town."

She didn't smile. "Window shopping for what? Tractor tires?"

They checked out in the motel office. "Y'all come back now," the woman behind the counter drawled, sounding like an exaggerated movie version of a southerner.

"I don't think so," James muttered under his breath.

Carrying his bag, he followed Christina out to the front. Then they made their way along the asphalt lot to the back where they had parked the car.

The sky, which had started out clear and sunny, had grown overcast. A wall of high gray clouds floated overhead from the south. The air was hot and damp.

"Looks like rain," James muttered.

They turned the corner of the building and stopped.

Christina grabbed James's arm and uttered a silent gasp. "The car — " she said, holding onto him tightly, her face pale and wide-eyed with surprise. "The car — it's gone!"

Chapter 17

Dropping their bags against the back of the building, they walked to the spot where the car had been parked. Christina stared down at a large spot of black oil, as if it might give a clue as to where the car had gone.

"I don't believe it," she whispered, shaking her head, still staring at the oil stain.

"Terri must have taken it," James said, his voice shaking.

Christina gazed up at him. He looks really frightened, she thought. He's trying to come on brave and cool, but he looks scared to death.

"She couldn't have taken it," Christina told him. She opened her bag and fumbled around in it. After a brief search, she pulled out a keychain. "I have the keys," she announced grimly. "Terri couldn't have taken the car without the keys."

She watched James's mouth drop open in surprise. "That's the only pair?" he asked, staring at them.

She nodded. "Yep."

He kicked at a pebble on the asphalt surface, sending it bouncing into the back of the building. "Guess we *have* to call the police," he said quietly.

"We *have* to get *out* of here," Christina urged, squeezing his hand. "Someone is *after* us, James. If someone took Terri and the car, they'll be coming after us next."

"What are you saying?" He squinted at her, his confusion revealed on his face. "Just run away?"

"We *have* to!" she cried shrilly. Her eyes watered up, and two tears slid down her hot cheeks. "I can't take this! I can't!"

"But, Christina — " he started, reaching for her.

She pulled back, out of his reach. "We're in danger here! Real danger! We have to get as far away as we can!" Her entire body was trembling now.

"But the car — " James started.

"I don't *care* about the car!" she screamed, feeling herself slip out of control. "I don't care about the car — and there's nothing you and I can do about Terri! Not if some crazy person is after us!"

"Okay, okay." James turned to see if anyone was watching them. "Just chill, all right? We'll go."

"Good," she replied, then uttered a loud sob. "Let's just get out of here." Two more tears rolled down her cheeks.

The sky darkened. The gray clouds seemed to lower over them. The wet air carried a chill.

Christina took a deep breath. The pungent aroma of diesel fuel filled her nostrils. "I hate this place. I really do," she cried.

They picked up their bags and made their way to the front.

"What are we going to do?" James asked, his eyes on the empty road that led through town.

"Hitch, I guess," she replied, keeping close by his side.

"Okay. You feel a little calmer?"

"Not really," she told him. "I won't feel calmer till we're away from here."

"Not much traffic," he said as they walked along the road, their sneakers crunching on the gravel.

The sky darkened to charcoal-gray. The wind gusted, blowing the cypress trees and pines along the road.

"We'll just keep walking north," she said. "Someone will come along eventually."

A red pickup truck carrying a load of tree stumps rolled past.

"Hope it doesn't rain," James said, gazing up at the threatening sky. "Hope it blows over. Otherwise, we'll get drenched."

"I don't care," Christina replied, shifting her bag to the other hand. Another pickup truck, this one empty, rumbled by. "As long as we get away."

They stopped at the one coffee shop in town and had coffee and jelly doughnuts at the counter. Christina normally hated the bitter taste of coffee. But this morning it tasted good, and the warmth of it helped to calm her a little.

After breakfast, they made their way through the small town, past the tiny post office and the farm equipment store and a sad-looking general store with a beat-up, old dentist chair out in front of it, for some reason.

A short while later, they were trudging along the side of the highway, turning at every sound to raise their thumbs and wait expectantly for someone to stop.

There were mostly trucks on the road this early. The few cars that came by didn't even slow down.

The sky became a drab olive color. Christina felt a few cold raindrops on her forehead.

"Hey — look!" James pointed to a car approaching rapidly from the other direction. "Is that your Honda?"

"Huh?" Christina gaped in shock.

The blue Honda roared by. There were two women in the front seat.

"No," Christina told him, lowering her head unhappily. "No way. That was a Civic, I think. You know, the smaller model."

"It was the same color," James said defensively. He was a few feet ahead of her. He stopped and waited for her to catch up.

"We've walked pretty far," she said, sounding discouraged.

"There are more cars now," he replied. "Someone will stop."

"Feel those raindrops?" she asked.

"I still don't believe it about Terri," he said, slowing his pace to stay beside her.

"I know," she said, frowning. "If only — "

"I mean, she was fine when I left her. She seemed in a perfectly good mood."

"Huh?" Christina cried out in surprise. She tossed her bag down on the sandy ground. "What do you *mean*?"

He stared back at her, obviously bewildered. "Just what I said. When I left her — "

Christina swallowed hard. It took her a while to speak. "You were with her last night? Why didn't you tell me? You *saw* her?"

"Well, yeah," James said. "We went for a walk. I was sure she told you."

"She didn't tell me *anything*," Christina said heatedly. Her eyes peered accusingly into James's. "She told me she was going out to get some fresh air. She didn't tell me she was meeting you."

The rain started to come down harder, spattering noisily against the surface of the highway.

"She knocked on my door," James explained, ignoring the rain. "She said she wanted to apologize. We went for a walk. In the woods behind the motel. We talked a bit. Then we came back."

"No, you didn't!" Christina accused heatedly, her eyes wide with anger — and fear. "You didn't come back with her."

"Huh?" James stared at her, confused. "Yes, I did. I walked her back to the motel."

"You took her to the woods," Christina accused, fear tightening her features, narrowing her eyes as she glared at him. "You took Terri to the woods, but you didn't bring her back. She never came back to the room."

"Whoa. Hold on, girl." James dropped his bag and reached for her.

"*Stay away from me!*" Christina shrieked.

"Christina!"

"I *mean* it! Stay away from me!" She took a step back from him, then another. Her T-shirt was splotched with rain. Her hair was already drenched. She didn't seem to notice.

"Listen," he said calmly, staring into her eyes. "You're getting all crazy. I didn't — "

"Where is she, James?" Christina demanded coldly. "Where is Terri? What did you *do* to her last night?"

Chapter 18

James made no attempt to answer Christina's questions. He stared at her intently, as if trying to decide what his next move should be.

Christina eyed him coldly, accusingly. But her hard expression quickly softened to reveal her fear. Her entire body convulsed in a violent shudder as the terror of her situation settled over her.

"Christina — " James started.

But she cut him off by raising her hand. "No more lies," she said, her voice barely above a whisper.

The rain picked up, swirled by gusts of cold wind.

Christina turned her eyes down the road, which curved into the tall pines to the left. Two crows sat side by side on the high telephone wires across the highway, bobbing and swaying in the wind.

James reached out to her, but she backed away, her face revealing anger and fear. "Don't touch me!" she cried shrilly. "I mean it, James."

"Listen to me," he demanded impatiently, his eyes narrowing as he glared at her. His rain-soaked T-shirt clung to his body. His hair was drenched, and rivulets of rain water ran down his cheeks.

Christina shook her head violently. "I can't believe I let this happen to me," she said, not really speaking to him but talking aloud to herself. "I can't believe I'm here all alone, in the middle of nowhere, on this empty highway — with *you*."

He shot her an angry look, angry and desperate at the same time. "You didn't feel that way about me yesterday," he said.

She tugged at her wet hair. "I didn't know. I didn't think. I thought that Terri — "

James started to say something, but stopped.

The first gunshot made them both cry out.

At the *crack* of the second gunshot, they both dove to the wet, sandy ground.

Chapter 19

Huddled next to Christina, James raised his head, then warily lifted himself to his knees.

"Who is it?" Christina cried, her head buried in her hands. "Who is shooting at us?"

"I don't see anyone," James replied, his eyes surveying the thick pine trees. "It's hard to see through the rain, but — "

"What? What is it?" Christina cried.

James shielded his eyes with one hand and stared at the woods to their right as two men stepped out from the trees. Both were wearing khaki trousers and green-and-brown army camouflage jackets. Both wore bright orange baseball caps.

Both were carrying rifles.

James rose quickly to his feet, balling his fists as if preparing for a fight.

Christina reluctantly stood up beside him, clutched her small suitcase, and raised it in front of her like a shield.

The two men, holding their rifles straight up at their sides, approached quickly, their boots squishing noisily over the wet, sandy ground.

"Did we scare you?" one of them called.

"Hey — we didn't see you," his companion added.

Christina and James remained frozen in place as the two men came up to them. "Hunters," James muttered, making a face.

"We were after quail," the taller one said, grinning sheepishly at Christina. "We didn't mean to flush you out."

"You okay?" his companion asked.

James nodded. "Yeah. It was just a flesh wound," he joked sarcastically.

"We thought you were shooting at us," Christina said shakily, still holding up the suitcase.

"What are you two doing out here?" the first hunter asked, keeping his eyes on her.

"Yeah. Don't you know enough to come in out of the rain?" the other one added with a loud snort. "Or are you as dumb as Earl and me?"

Both hunters snorted loudly, grinning at Christina.

"We're pretty dumb," James replied, hands on his hips, still eyeing them suspiciously.

"We're just trying to hitch a ride north," Christina said, avoiding their eyes.

Why are they staring at me like that? Christina thought. Why are they grinning at me?

She felt a tremor of fear.

They both had rifles. If they tried anything, she and James would be helpless.

Even James with his wild temper wouldn't be

much of a match for these two burly men with hunting rifles.

"Not much traffic on this road so early," the taller one said, turning his eyes to the highway.

"You might get lucky," the other one offered, still gazing at Christina.

"Yeah. Some driver is bound to feel sorry for you in this rain," the first one agreed. "You both look so pitiful."

They both snorted with laughter again.

The taller one raised his rifle in both hands.

Again, Christina felt a tremor of fear.

But he quickly lowered the gun onto his shoulder. "Sorry again," he said, his grin fading.

"Yeah. Sorry," his companion repeated. "Good luck."

They both turned and headed back toward the trees, taking long strides over the sandy ground.

Christina stood holding her suitcase, staring after them until they disappeared into the woods. "They really scared me," she said in a dull, flat voice, not looking at James.

"They weren't so bad," James said. He raked his hand back through his wet hair and turned to Christina. "Now, if you'd just listen to me for one second."

She scowled at him. "I want to know the truth, James. The truth about Terri."

She saw that he was suddenly staring past her. She turned to see a car approaching.

James stepped onto the road and raised his thumb. Christina stepped beside him, shivering from the cold rain.

The car drew closer. It was a white car, she saw. An Oldsmobile, maybe.

James waved his hand, signaling the car to stop.

It sped past.

The tires sent up a mist of rainwater behind it. The driver was alone inside.

James lowered his hand, his expression dejected.

The car squealed to a stop, sliding over the wet pavement.

James stared at it as if not believing his eyes.

The car backed up, then stopped about twenty yards ahead of them.

"Hey — a ride!" Christina cried happily.

James grabbed up his canvas bag and ran after her toward the white car.

The side windows were steamed up. The driver rolled down the front passenger window. "Where you kids headed?"

"North," Christina told him, leaning into the window.

He was a young man, she saw, with short brown hair, thinning in front. He wore black-rimmed glasses. He was dressed in a yellow-and-white-striped polo shirt and faded jeans.

"I'll pop the trunk," he said. "Throw your stuff in there."

The trunk popped open. Christina and James immediately stowed their bags, slammed the trunk shut, then hurried to get in out of the rain. Christina climbed into the front seat. James lowered himself into the back.

"Bad day to be hitching," the man said, wiping

the steam off the windshield with a wadded-up tissue. "How'd you kids get all the way out here?"

"Just lucky," James said sarcastically.

"Thanks for stopping," Christina said gratefully, wiping water off her eyebrows with her hand. "We thought no one would stop for us."

The man smiled and stuck out his hand for her to shake. "My name's Art," he said cheerily. He pulled his hand away quickly. "Man, you're really soaked."

Christina and James introduced themselves.

"I'm heading to Atlanta," Art told them, shifting into drive and heading the car back onto the road. "That should give you time to dry off. Where you coming from?"

"Florida," Christina replied. "It was school break. So we went to Fort Lauderdale."

"Just the two of you?" He accelerated, and the car hummed, the speedometer rising quickly to fifty.

"No. My friend Terri and me," Christina said. "My other friend, I mean."

Art nodded thoughtfully, his eyes on the road.

The windshield wipers clicked in rhythm as the gray world whirred by on both sides. Christina settled back and closed her eyes, trying to relax.

"I'm going to cut over to the main highway up here," Art said, slowing as the road curved sharply to the left. "Then it's straight ahead to Atlanta."

"This is real nice of you," James said, rubbing away the steam with his hand so he could see out his window.

"Hey, I had to stop," Art replied. "I couldn't let you *drown* out there, could I?" He smiled at Christina. "Besides, I could use the company. The radio's busted, so it was too quiet."

The green highway marker loomed on the right. A short while later, Art maneuvered the car onto the four-lane highway and sped up to sixty.

The rain continued to pour down. The wipers slid rapidly, but didn't seem to accomplish much. The car in front of them sprayed a tidal wave of water onto the windshield.

Glancing in his rearview mirror, Art changed lanes. "Low visibility day," he muttered. "I usually like the rain. Good for the crops and all that. But I hate to drive in it."

"I know what you mean," James replied awkwardly. "You live in Atlanta?"

Art shook his head. "No. Down south. How about you?"

"Well, I'm from Key West," James told him. "But I'm thinking of moving."

"Key West is so touristy," Art said, making a face.

James agreed.

They rode on in silence for a while.

James turned his eyes to Christina. She was sitting tensely in the front passenger seat, hands clasped tightly in her lap, staring straight ahead, chewing on her lower lip.

He settled back against the warmth of the seat-back and closed his eyes. Her angry accusations repeated themselves in his mind. He thought about

Terri, about their walk together the night before in the pine woods.

Terri. Terri. Terri. The name repeated itself in his thoughts, repeated endlessly until it became a meaningless chant.

Christina's alarmed voice broke through his thoughts.

"That sign! Art — it said we're going south!"

Art didn't reply.

James leaned forward, squinting to see out through the clouded windshield. The sign had whirred past. Now he could see only trees and endless, flat fields.

Outside, the rain had lightened. The clouds hovered low in the sky, as if closing in on the speeding car.

"We're going in the wrong direction," Christina said shrilly. "We're going south."

"I know," Art said quietly, eyes straight ahead, his expression blank.

"But — why? What's going on here?" Christina demanded.

"Yeah, what's the deal?" James chimed in from the back seat. He put a hand on Art's shoulder. "You said you were heading north."

"I lied," Art said flatly.

"Huh?" James reacted with surprise.

"Where are we going? What do you *mean*?" Christina asked, fear tightening her throat.

"A little detour," Art said, still showing no emotion. He jerked his shoulder out from James's grasp, and stepped down on the gas.

"Where are you taking us?" James asked.

"Something I want to show you," Art replied. A strange smile spread slowly on his face.

"Let us out!" Christina screamed. "Stop the car." She pulled up the door handle, but the door was locked.

"We don't want any trouble," James said softly.

Art didn't reply.

"Stop the car!" Christina screamed, her features twisted in panic.

Ignoring her pleas, Art stared straight ahead into the gray glare. He reached his right hand to the dashboard and fumbled with the dials. "Where is the defroster?" he asked, speaking to himself. "I really hate these rental cars."

"This isn't your car?" James asked. "It's a rental?"

"Well, I knew you'd recognize the blue Taurus," Art replied matter-of-factly. "So I rented this car after I left you last night."

Chapter 20

"Let us out! Let us *out!*" Christina shrieked, her eyes wide with panic.

Uttering an angry cry, she reached out and grabbed the steering wheel.

Art hit the brake.

The car jolted hard, the tires skidding on the slick pavement.

Car horns honked.

James was jerked forward. His head hit the headrest on Christina's seat. Then he was tossed back against his own seat.

He looked up in time to see Art elbow Christina hard, shoving her back toward her side.

She cried out in pain, and her hands flew off the wheel.

A blue van to their left swerved sharply as Art struggled to get the car back in the lane.

More horns honked.

"That was stupid," Art said, breathing hard, glancing angrily at Christina.

"I don't get this," James said, thinking hard,

trying to figure out his best move. "I really don't get this."

"I'll bet you don't," Art said quietly, narrowing his eyes as he glanced at James in the rearview mirror.

Christina grabbed the door handle again. She turned to pull up the door lock.

Art reached over with his right hand. He grabbed her shoulder and swung her back.

"Let me out!" Christina screamed. She began waving wildly at the driver of the blue van.

Keeping his left hand on the wheel, Art reached under the seat. When his right hand emerged, it was holding a small, silver pistol.

"Now maybe we can all calm down," he said.

Christina gasped. "Are you going to shoot us?"

"I don't want to," Art said. "I really don't want to." He took his eyes off the road to stare at her. "It's really up to you."

"What do you want?" James asked Art, placing a hand on Christina's trembling shoulder.

Art frowned and didn't reply.

"Everybody just settle down. Enjoy the ride," he said. He drove with one hand, holding the gun tightly in the other, which he rested on his lap.

"We're back in Florida," Christina wailed, smearing the clouded window with her hand so that she could read the passing signs.

"The sunshine state," Art said quietly. "And, look, the clouds are lifting."

He switched off the windshield wipers. The clouds were still hovering darkly, but appeared to be pulling apart. A patch of blue sky poked through low on the horizon.

"Why did you follow us last night?" James demanded, leaning forward, his hand still on Christina's shoulder. "What do you want? Do you want money? We don't have any money."

"Shut up and sit back," Art snapped, raising the pistol. "Enough talk. Everyone just shut up."

James obediently let go of Christina's shoulder and slid back in his seat.

Christina uttered a loud sigh. "Let us go. Please. We won't tell anyone about this. Really."

Art slammed the side of the gun hard against the dashboard, startling Christina and James. "I said shut up."

Christina let out a short cry of protest, but didn't say anything. James edged back in the seat, thinking hard, trying to figure out a plan to get them out of this jam.

Maybe I'd better wait till we get out of the car, he thought.

But where is he taking us?

And who *is* he? James wondered. What does he want with us? Is he just a kidnapper? Why on earth would he want to kidnap *us*? Don't kidnappers only kidnap rich kids so they can get a big ransom?

No, James decided. This isn't a simple kidnapping.

But what *is* it?

He turned sideways in the seat and studied Art. He isn't that big, James thought. He doesn't look like he works out or anything. I can probably take him.

Yes. I can definitely take him.

The pistol is a problem. But not that big of a problem.

I just have to wait for the right moment.

They continued making their way south. The highway was dry there. The clouds gave way to blue skies. The afternoon sun beamed down from directly above. The air inside the car became hot and uncomfortable.

Christina sat stiffly, staring out the side window, her hands tightly knotted in her lap. Her hair was disheveled. Several long curls had fallen over her eyes, but she made no attempt to brush them aside.

"Where are you taking us?" she asked in a soft, trembling voice, breaking several minutes of silence.

"You'll see," Art replied, the gun still clenched tightly in his hand.

He slowed to turn off the highway.

I can jump out, James thought, his muscles tensing. He reached for the door handle.

The car slowed even more to make the turn.

James took a deep breath.

Then hesitated.

He removed his hand from the handle and settled back.

Art maneuvered the car along a narrow road that led through thick forests on both sides. Picking up speed, the car bumped and bounced over the potholed road.

The air grew steamy and wet. There wasn't another car in sight. James recognized beech trees and cypresses, and weeping willows that seemed to bend sadly onto the road.

We're heading into swamplands, James realized. Upraised tree roots rose up from thickly puddled mud. Vines hung down over the wet, leafy underbrush. A one-lane bridge carried them over a dried-up pond.

"Almost home," Art said, talking to himself. He glanced at Christina. "I hope you like my little swamp cabin. Actually, it belongs to a friend. But I know he won't mind if we make use of it." And then he added ominously, "We won't be using it long."

Christina turned to check on James. Her eyes were wide with terror. Her lower lip was trembling.

James raised a finger to his lips, as if to say, "Shhhh. Don't worry."

But as Art pulled the car onto an unpaved path that led through the trees, James felt a cold shiver of fear that started at the back of his neck and ran down his entire body.

Cold, paralyzing terror.

Back there in the thick swamp with no one around for miles, Art could do whatever he wanted to them. And there was no hope of anyone coming to their rescue.

No hope at all.

The car began to climb as the dirt road sloped up. The trees were so thick and tangled that it grew dark as evening, with only occasional rays of sunlight able to penetrate the leafy overhead covering.

"Ow!" Christina cried out as the car hit a deep hole in the road.

Art laughed out loud.

He pulled the car to a stop in front of a small, clapboard cabin. "Home sweet home," he said, turning to Christina. "Look how nice and private it is. No neighbors at all. No nosy neighbors to interfere with our . . . party."

"What are you going to do?" Christina demanded, sounding more frightened than angry.

Art raised the gun and waved it toward Christina's car door. "Get out."

Christina hesitated.

He pulled the gun back, threatening to hit her with it.

She swallowed hard and reached for the door handle.

"You, too," Art called back to James.

A few seconds later, all three of them were standing outside the car, staring at the small, flat-roofed cabin. It wasn't much bigger than a shed.

Peering in through the one window, James saw that it was dark inside.

An aluminum bucket, half-filled with rainwater, stood tilted by the front door. Several crushed beer cans littered the dirt in front of the cabin. A fishing rod without a reel leaned against one wall.

Art kicked a beer can across the dirt. "Looks like my friend has been here recently," he said, his face expressionless.

He turned, yawning loudly, and stretched, arching his back and raising both hands above his head. "Oooh, long drive."

This is my chance, James thought, feeling his muscles tense.

His back is turned. I can catch him off-guard.

I can tackle him to the ground.

I can take him.

James hesitated for only a brief moment.

Then, with a running start, he leapt at Art's back.

Chapter 21

As he made his jump, James raised his arms to tackle Art.

But Art wheeled around quickly and swung his knee up, driving it deep into James's stomach.

"Uhh."

The impact sent the air rushing out of James's lungs.

Pain shot through him, shocking him, crippling him in midair.

As he dropped to his knees, James struggled to suck in fresh air.

But the pain was too much. He couldn't breathe in or out.

It hurt too much. Everything hurt. Even his eyelids hurt.

He knew he was going down.

Down, down, down.

Everything was so bright.

And then so dark.

* * *

James opened his eyes.

It was still so dark.

He blinked. Once. Twice. Things started to come into focus.

He was inside the cabin, he realized. Pale light flickered in from the only window.

He tried to stand up. But something held him back.

"Christina?" he called.

She was beside him, seated in a stiff-backed wooden chair. Art stood behind her, unwrapping a length of white cord in his hands.

I'm tied up, James realized.

He was in a matching straight-backed chair, his hands tied behind his back. Cord wrapped tightly around his waist.

"Hey!" he called. He didn't recognize his own voice. It sounded muffled. Far away.

"You're back among the living?" Art asked, a grin spreading across his narrow face. His eyeglasses glinted from the sunlight pouring in through the window. They appeared to be lighted up, almost aflame.

"What's going on?" James managed to ask. His stomach ached. He could feel his pulse throbbing in his wrists. The cord was so tight.

"You made a very stupid move," Art said matter-of-factly, "and you paid for it."

"Don't tie me up. Please!" Christina begged.

Art ignored her. Holding a section of the cord taut, he moved in front of her. "Hold out your hands."

"Please!" Christina begged, her voice shrill, about to burst into tears. "Please!"

"Hold out your hands," Art repeated patiently.

"Listen, we haven't done anything to you," James told him. "Why are you doing this?"

"Hold your hands together," Art instructed Christina.

She reluctantly held out her hands. They were trembling. James saw that her whole body was shaking.

Then, suddenly, Christina's expression changed. She gazed into Art's eyes. "Listen, Art, I'll do something really nice for you if you let us go," she said in a breathy voice.

Art hesitated. "What did you say?"

"I said I have something nice for you." Christina's voice was teasing, almost playful. "I'll give it to you if you let us go. It'll be worth it, Art. Really. It will."

"Christina — what are you *saying*?" James exclaimed.

Chapter 22

Art stared thoughtfully at Christina. "Do I look stupid to you?" he asked.

Christina's mouth dropped open. "Huh?"

"Do I look stupid to you?" he repeated. "First your pal here tries to drop me from behind. Then you start coming on to me. I'm not stupid. I — "

"I'm not coming on to you," Christina protested. "I'm serious. I have something I'll give you if you let James and me go."

"What?" Art asked, leaning over her menacingly.

"Money," Christina replied. She glanced at James, then quickly looked away.

"Money? Where would *you* get money?" Art asked skeptically.

"I have it. A lot," Christina told him. "Let us go. I'll give it all to you."

Art snapped the cord between his hands. "You're lying."

"No. Really. I'm not," Christina protested.

Art leaned over her. "I'm warning you . . ."

James closed his eyes, thinking hard.

He knew Christina had no money. She had told him so.

What was she talking about? What was her plan?

Was she just stalling for time? If so, it was stupid. She was just going to make Art angrier than he already was.

James opened his eyes. The light from the window dimmed, casting the small room in shadow. In the darker light, the white cord between Art's hands appeared to glow.

Outside, trees whispered and bent.

The only sound, James thought.

The only sound for miles.

We're all alone here. All alone. And Christina's trying to bribe her way out with money she doesn't have.

James let his eyes wander rapidly about the cabin. He was searching for a weapon. Anything. Anything he might be able to use on Art if he got the chance.

But except for a square wooden table and the two chairs he and Christina were sitting on, and a stack of yellowing newspapers in the corner, the cabin was bare.

"Show me the money," Art told Christina, staring at her hard, trying to determine if she was telling the truth.

"Do you promise to let us go?" Christina asked, again glancing at James.

"Yeah. Okay," Art replied. "If it's enough money."

"It's in my bag," Christina said. She pointed to

the car outside the window. "In the trunk." She stood up. "Shall I go get it?"

Art grabbed her shoulders and pushed her down roughly. "Don't trouble yourself. I'll go," he said. He turned his eyes to James. "Remember, I still have a gun. Don't either of you make a move. I'm real serious. *Real* serious. Can't you tell?"

He strode quickly across the small, dark room and out the door.

James turned to Christina and whispered, "I don't get it. What are you doing?"

"Maybe he'll let us go," Christina whispered back.

"But you don't have any money — " James started.

Art returned, carrying Christina's small suitcase. He dropped it heavily onto her lap. "Show me the money. You'd better not be lying."

"I'm not," Christina insisted. Her hand was shaking as she unzipped the lid to the suitcase.

What does she think she's doing? James wondered. This is only going to make Art even madder.

Christina fumbled through the wadded-up clothing in the bag. "Here," she said. She held up a brown wallet.

James stared at the wallet, bewildered.

"There's nearly a thousand dollars in here," Christina told Art.

He snatched the wallet from her hand.

"Go ahead. Count it," she said.

James's mouth dropped open. He turned to Christina, an expression of disbelief on his face. "It's

Paul's wallet!" he cried. "You stole my cousin's wallet!"

"Shut up," she snapped. "He had no business leaving it out like that."

"No *wonder* you and Terri thought it was Paul who was following us!" James said, shaking his head.

"Shut up. Just shut up," Christina warned sharply.

"Yeah. It's a thousand bucks," Art said, folding the wad of bills in half and tucking them into his trouser pocket. He tossed the wallet across the cabin.

"You can have it," Christina told him, staring defiantly at James.

"I don't *believe* this," James muttered.

"I already have it," Art said, smiling.

"So you'll let us go?" Christina asked hopefully.

"Sure. Okay. You can go," Art said.

Chapter 23

"We can go?" Christina asked uncertainly. She started to pull herself to her feet.

An unpleasant smile formed on Art's face. His eyes danced alertly behind his glasses. He stood poised in the center of the cabin, waiting for Christina to make a move.

"You were lying," Christina said, lowering her eyes in disappointment, long corkscrew curls falling over her face.

"Yeah. I was lying," Art replied, pleased with himself. "But thanks for the extra cash. I might not have found it when I went through your stuff later."

"Later? What are you going to do to us?" Christina asked, raising her head to stare at him, her expression as lifeless as her voice.

He shrugged in reply.

"Did you really think I would let you go?" he asked, taunting her now. "Did you really think I was that stupid?"

"No," Christina sobbed. "I mean yes. I mean — "

"Did you really think that a thousand dollars is enough to pay for what you did?" Art asked, leaning over Christina, lowering his face close to hers.

"What?" Christina cried. "What did *I* do? *Tell me!*"

He glared at her, breathing hard, but didn't reply.

James silently worked his hands behind his back, trying to loosen the cord. But his actions only made the cord tighter. It cut painfully into his wrists. He stopped, uttering a defeated sigh, and let his body go slack.

Art picked up the length of cord and pulled it taut between his hands. "Put your hands behind your back," he instructed Christina, taking a step back, lowering his voice, forcing back his anger.

Christina didn't move. She kept her hands on the sides of the chair bottom. She glared up at Art. "Just tell us why you're doing this," she demanded.

"Hands behind your back," Art repeated, snapping the cord loudly in front of her.

Christina shook her head. "I want to know why you've done this. Why did you follow us? Why did you kidnap us? Why?"

"I think you know," Art said, his anger seething once again to the surface. "Hands!" he shouted.

Seeing him begin to lose his temper, Christina felt a wave of fear sweep over her. She obediently clasped her hands behind her back.

Art moved behind the chair and quickly began wrapping the white cord around her wrists. "Don't you ever brush your hair?" he asked her.

"It'll be a little hard with my hands tied," she shot back. But then her voice revealed her fear. "Aren't you going to answer my question? Aren't you going to tell us what this is all about?"

"I think you know," he said again, knotting the cord.

Bright sunlight angled in through the window, and the room brightened. The light seemed to point to a small stove against the back wall of the cabin. On top of it, James spotted a metal cooking pot.

A weapon, he thought.

If only I could free myself.

Keeping his back straight, James tried once again to move his hands. But the pain from the tight cord was too sharp. Again he gave up, staring at the heavy pot, so near, almost within reach, yet so far.

"I think you know why you're here," Art repeated, backing to the center of the cabin, his eyes locked on Christina's.

"Please," she cried. "Why do you keep saying that? I have no idea. Really." A single tear rolled down her cheek. She stared back at Art through tangled curls.

Art's expression turned angry. His face reddened. His hands balled into tight fists at his sides.

"Do I have to give you a hint?" he screamed, losing control. "Do I?"

"Just tell us — " Christina started.

"Here's a hint!" he cried. "My name is Art Eckridge. Does that mean anything to you?"

"No!" Christina cried. She shook her head. "No, no, no!"

"Art Eckridge!" Art repeated, screaming his name.

"No. I don't *know* you!" Christina insisted, tears rolling down her cheeks.

"Well, I know *you!*" Art declared, advancing on her. "You and your friend. You're the ones who killed my father!"

Chapter 24

Art is insane, James thought. He's crazy. Messed up.

"You killed my father."

The words sent a chill down James's back.

We're not dealing with a rational person here, he realized. We're dealing with a psycho.

Art has totally lost it. He's out of his mind.

There's no way we'll be able to reason with him.

"Roger Eckridge!" Art bellowed at Christina. "Roger Eckridge! Roger Eckridge!"

Christina shut her eyes and cringed, trying to edge away from the shouted words.

"Now do you know why you're here?" Art screamed, his eyes bulging behind the glasses, his face tomato red.

"No!" Christina insisted, violently shaking her head. "I don't know that name. I don't know you! You're wrong!"

"Roger Eckridge!" Art screamed again. "You killed him! You and your friend!"

"I didn't kill anybody!" James protested.

"Not you," Art said, turning toward James, a startled look on his face, as if he had forgotten James was there. "Not you. Her. And her girlfriend." He pointed wildly at Christina.

"Terri?" Christina cried. "What do you know about Terri?"

"I already took care of Terri," Art said, still breathing hard but lowering his voice.

Christina uttered a loud sob.

"You've made a mistake," James said, trying to keep his voice low and steady. "You have the wrong people. It's just a mix-up. If someone killed your father — "

"*She* and her friend killed my father," Art said, shaking his finger at Christina.

"No!" Christina protested. "You're wrong!" She turned frantically to James. Her glance said: What are we going to do? How can we convince him that he's made a mistake?

James stared back at her in bewilderment.

He felt cold all over. His wrists ached. His hands tingled sharply. The cord had cut off their circulation.

Art is crazy.

The phrase repeated itself in James's mind.

He is crazy. And we're going to die.

"I warned Dad so many times not to pick up hitchhikers," Art said, sounding excited but not angry now. He walked to the window, turned, and lowered himself onto the windowsill, blocking most of the sunlight, casting the cabin in shadow.

"Art. Listen — " Christina started.

"I warned Dad," Art repeated, ignoring Christina's plea. "I told him time and again that it just wasn't safe to stop for people these days. But Dad wouldn't listen. Dad always wanted to believe the best in people. Even with all the news stories, all the horror stories every day in the newspaper, Dad wanted to believe that people were good, that people were brought up to be nice to each other."

Art reached into his pants pocket and removed the small silver pistol. It caught the sunlight from the window as he raised it, sending a ray of light darting around the small cabin.

The light flashed in James's eyes. He shut them.

If only I could shut my eyes, then open them and this would all be gone, James thought sadly.

But when he opened his eyes, everything was the same. Art still sat against the low windowsill, slapping the pistol now against his palm.

"A thousand times I told Dad not to pick up hitchhikers," Art continued. "But it was a habit he couldn't break. You see, Dad was kind. That's a word you don't hear very much these days. Kind." He glared at Christina. "You probably don't know that word, do you!"

Christina's cheeks were pale and wet from her silent tears. "Art, let us help you," she begged. "Let us help you get to the police. They'll find the ones who *really* killed your father."

"Yeah, Dad was kind," Art continued. He didn't seem to hear Christina. He seemed to be in his own world, staring at the floorboards as he talked.

"He believed in helping people," Art said "He

believed we all had to look out for one another. That's why he always stopped for hitchhikers. He said hitchhikers always look so lonely, so desperate, so needy. That's why Dad couldn't pass them by. That's why he picked *you* up," he said, turning his eyes to Christina. "You and your girlfriend."

"It wasn't us!" Christina cried, struggling to free her hands. "You have to believe me. It wasn't us!"

Art's face twisted into a menacing snarl.

"Listen to me!" Christina pleaded. "Give me a chance! It wasn't Terri and me. It was James! James killed your father! I *know* he did!"

Chapter 25

"James killed your father!" Christina screamed.

"Whoa!" James uttered an astonished cry.

He turned to Christina, but she avoided his gaze.

"You've got to believe me, Art. James *told* me the whole story. James *told* me how he killed your father!"

Art jumped to his feet.

Christina cried out, startled by the sudden move.

Art took a step toward James. Then another.

"Hey, this is *crazy*!" James cried. He stared at Christina. "Christina — what are you *doing*? Why did you say that?"

"Because it's true," Christina snapped back. "Tell him, James. Tell Art how you hitched a ride with his dad and how you killed him. Tell Art the story you told me."

Art took another step toward James, his expression dark and menacing.

"Christina — you liar!" James cried, his throat choked with panic.

"You believe me — *don't* you, Art?" Christina

asked. "James confessed everything to me. You believe me — right, Art?"

"I don't believe you," Art said softly. He raised the gun waist-high in front of him.

"But James told me!" Christina insisted shrilly.

"I don't believe you because I was there," Art said quietly. "I was there, Christina, and I saw you and your girlfriend."

"No! That's impossible. It was James — " Christina started.

But Art silenced her with a wave of his pistol.

She gasped and snapped back in the chair as if she had been shot. "You were there?"

Art nodded, holding the gun poised.

Clouds drifted over the sun again. Shadows lengthened over the cabin. Darkness swept over everything.

"Dad was heading home," Art said, scratching his temple with the barrel of the pistol. "I was driving to visit him. Driving toward you. I saw you and your girlfriend push him out of the car. You dumped him onto the side of the highway and drove off. I wanted to go after you. But I had to stop and take care of Dad."

"No!" Christina cried. "No! No! No!" She shook her head violently, her eyes closed.

Is she denying it? James wondered. Or does she just want Art to stop accusing her?

"No! No! No!"

"Yes," Art insisted. "I was there. I saw you. I saw Terri. You killed my father. You dumped him onto the highway and stole his car."

"No! No!" Christina tossed her head back against the wooden chairback. Her eyes were closed, and her features were twisted in agony.

"Terri told me everything," Art continued, ignoring Christina's reaction. "Terri confessed to everything. This morning. Before I took care of her."

"Took care of her?" James asked, his voice muffled by fear.

"Before I punished her for her crime," Art said, keeping his eyes on Christina. He lowered the pistol and cradled it in both hands.

Christina's shoulders heaved, and her body convulsed with a loud sob.

"I guess you're going to tell me how sorry you are," Art said dryly.

"I didn't mean to kill him!" Christina blurted out, large tears glistening down her cheeks, staining her T-shirt.

James swallowed hard.

I don't believe this, he thought.

All the time I was riding with Terri and Christina and we were listening to the radio and hearing all those news reports about the old man being killed by a hitchhiker — all the time the girls knew that *they* had been the ones who did it.

He leaned forward, wriggling his hands, trying to get the blood flowing, trying to make them stop tingling.

His mind filled with whirling images. He could picture Christina and Terri pushing the old man out the car door, then speeding away. Then he pictured

Christina stealing his cousin Paul's wallet.

I've been such a jerk, James thought.

I came along with them. I was so knocked out by Christina. I even thought she cared about me.

I thought I was a tough guy. I thought I knew what was going down.

And all the while . . .

A wave of anger descended over him, tightening his muscles, building, building — until he wanted to scream.

I've been such a jerk. Such a stupid jerk.

"I didn't mean to kill him," Christina was telling Art, her voice trembling with emotion, her eyes filled with fear. "You have to believe me. I didn't mean to hit the old guy that hard. My hand just slipped, that's all. His head — it cracked. I mean, I didn't want to — "

Her voice caught in her throat. She gasped for breath.

Art stood patiently over her, not saying a word, waiting for her to continue.

"Terri and I, we only wanted the car," Christina continued, still breathing hard, staring down at the floor as she spoke. "We were so tired of hitching. So tired of all the boys stopping and hitting on us, giving us a hard time.

"We had no money," she continued. "These boys we met in Lauderdale at the beach. They stole our money. Great guys, huh? Terri and I didn't have enough money to call home. And we were so tired."

"So you decided to take advantage of an old man," Art said bitterly.

Christina nodded. "But we didn't mean to kill him. You've got to believe that. We just wanted the car. We just wanted to get home. But the old man — I mean, your dad — "

"I got him to the hospital," Art said, staring down at Christina, the gun still cradled in both hands. "Then I headed north. I figured I'd find you sooner or later. I figured you'd be too dumb to dump the car."

Christina nodded sadly. "We should've gotten rid of it sooner. Terri and I argued about that. I told Terri we couldn't keep the car that long. But she was such a wimp. She kept insisting we could get away. . . ."

"Where is the car?" Art demanded angrily. He raised the pistol and took a step toward Christina. "Why were you hitching this morning? Where is my dad's car?"

"I — I hid it last night," Christina stammered.

"Huh?" James cried in surprise.

She turned to him. "I made Terri take you for a walk in the woods last night. I knew we had to dump the car. I knew that's why we were being followed. But I didn't want you to suspect anything. When you were safely off with Terri, I took the car and hid it."

James shook his head.

I can't believe it, he thought. I'm such a jerk. Such a jerk!

Christina's face suddenly brightened. She turned back to Art. "I'll take you to the car," she said.

Art stared down at her, studying her face. He didn't reply.

"I'll show you where it is," Christina insisted. "Untie me. I'll take you there. You want to get your father's car back, don't you?"

Art remained silent. His eyes appeared to glaze over. He lost all expression, as if he were deep in thought.

"I'll take you there," Christina repeated, sounding very desperate. "*Please!* Let me show you where the car is!"

Another long pause.

Finally, Art answered her. "No way," he said softly. "I've got *other* plans for you."

Chapter 26

"Dad was so kind," Art said. "So kind. He was like some kind of trusting animal, you know. Always looking for the good in people. Even when there wasn't any."

He gave Christina a hard shove in the back. She nearly lost her footing.

"Keep moving," Art instructed.

He had forced them out of the cabin, their hands still tied behind their backs, motioning with the pistol. He guided them onto a dirt path that led up a sloping hill through a tangle of trees and vines.

The sun was beginning to lower itself to their right. The air was still hot and sticky. Tiny white insects swarmed about their heads.

"Keep moving," Art urged impatiently, walking a few yards behind them, keeping the pistol trained on their backs. "I want to show you something interesting."

"Take us to the police — please!" Christina pleaded. She and James walked with their eyes to the ground, watching out for upraised tree roots that broke through the narrow path.

"Police aren't much good in these parts," Art said matter-of-factly. "Besides, they take too long. I tend to believe in quick justice."

"What do you mean?" Christina asked with a trembling voice.

"You'll see," Art said curtly. "Keep walking. It's just up on this bluff."

Where is he taking us? James wondered, raising his eyes from the ground occasionally to look around. Large, leafy vines grew over the dirt path. Behind them, barkless trees, their roots poking up through the mud, bent low, their sinuous branches twisting into each other, allowing only splotches of sunlight to filter through.

It's all swamp, James thought. What does he want to show us in a swamp?

Christina brushed against him as they climbed the path. She stared up at him, trying to exchange glances.

But James turned sharply away, scowling, and took long strides to get ahead of her.

She's played me for a sucker long enough, he told himself.

He thought of all the kisses. That night at Paul's house . . . in the back seat of the car as Terri drove . . .

And then, she tries to convince Art that *I'm* the one who killed his father.

I'm not your sucker anymore, Christina, James thought bitterly.

He swallowed hard. I'm probably going to *die* because of her, he realized.

The unfairness of it struck him all at once, nearly taking his breath away. He stopped in the middle of the path.

I'm going to die. For no reason.

No reason.

"Keep going," Art barked impatiently, waving the pistol. "All the way to the top."

White gnats buzzed around James's face. One flew into his eye. He couldn't raise his hands to get it out.

Christina again tried to signal to him, but he ignored her, walking a few steps ahead, stepping over a low vine stalk, shaking his head hard to try to discourage the gnats.

"A friend of mine owns all this," Art said, close behind, sounding a little out of breath. "That's his cabin back there. He and I use it sometimes when we go fishing."

Christina and James made no reply. The three of them were nearly at the top of the path.

"That's how I knew about this place," Art continued, as if they were having a conversation. He snickered. "You didn't think I just happened to come by it by accident, did you?"

Again, neither Christina nor James replied.

"No, my friend Jack and I, we use the cabin a lot. Of course, I never knew it would come in *this* handy."

Where is he taking us? James wondered, raising his eyes to the top of the hill.

It's just swamp and more swamp.

What could be so special up here? Is he just taking us here to shoot us? A hidden place way back in the swamp where we won't ever be found?

"Please!" Christina begged, stopping and turning back toward Art. "Please — the police."

"My friend Jack has a very unusual hobby," Art went on, almost jauntily.

"Please!"

"I don't know anyone else who has a hobby quite like this," Art said, motioning Christina forward with the pistol. "Anyone I ever bring here finds it quite amazing. Quite amazing."

"I have more money!" Christina pleaded. "I can *get* more money. *Lots* of it. From my parents. *Please.*"

"There are some things you expect to find back here," Art continued, a little more out of breath, "and there are some things you *don't* expect to find. Now, I've known Jack for a lot of years. We were in school together, you see. And all the time I've known him, he's always been a little squirrely. A little off-center."

"How much money do you want?" Christina cried. "I can get it for you. My parents are loaded. *Please!* Please, listen to me!"

"But this is a strange hobby, even for Jack," Art explained, stepping over a fallen tree limb. "Well, well. Here we are." Hè grinned at them. "We've gone as far as we can go."

The path ended abruptly, James saw. The trees

on either side just stopped. As if they had come to the end of the world.

The end of the world, James thought. I guess that's what this is.

"I can make you rich. Really, I can!" Christina persisted.

They were standing on the edge of a sharp precipice, James saw. He was hot and uncomfortable, perspiring from the climb. His wrists, bound so tightly, ached and throbbed.

Reluctantly he lowered his head and peered down.

There was water down below. A large, green-brown pond, shadows playing over the still water.

"Take a look," Art urged. "It's deeper than you think."

Christina shuddered and let out a short, frightened cry.

"Believe it or not, it's a freshwater pond," Art said, stepping up right behind Christina.

She turned, a look of terror on her face. He stared over her shoulder, looking down at the water.

"It has to be fresh water, you see, because of Jack's hobby," he said. "Take a look."

Christina and James obediently stared down.

The water was still and murky. James detected low ripples. Nothing more.

"Piranhas need fresh water," Art announced matter-of-factly. "That's why Jack needed to build his cabin near a freshwater pond. For his hobby. You see, Jack raises piranhas here. You've heard of piranhas?"

James nodded, but didn't reply. A cold chill coursed down his back as he began to realize what Art had in store for him and Christina.

"Please!" Christina whimpered.

"Piranhas are a very interesting hobby, don't you think?" Art asked jovially. "Jack keeps this little pond of his well-stocked. Well-stocked. Hey — see that one jump?"

"Please!" Christina begged. *"Please!"*

"I just have to criticize Jack for one tiny thing," Art continued, cruelly ignoring Christina's pleas. He continued to stare down over the sharp edge of the precipice. "Jack's a good ol' boy, but he has one fault. He just doesn't feed his pets enough. Hear what I'm saying? He keeps his piranhas real hungry. In fact, you might say he *starves* them."

James exhaled loudly.

Did he bring us here to talk us to death? he wondered angrily.

He's deliberately torturing us.

James tried once again to free his hands, but the cord cut into his wrists. He gasped loudly from the pain.

The sound made Art turn his attention to James. "Too bad about you, son," he said softly. "You sort of got caught up in a place you didn't belong."

"You going to let me go?" James asked, eyeing Art coldly.

Art shook his head. "Can't do that. Can I? There's a lesson here, son. A lesson about hanging out with the wrong kind of women. But I guess the lesson isn't going to do you much good."

"Please — " Christina repeated, whimpering, her shoulders heaving.

"Tell you what," Art said to James. "I'll give you a break."

"A break?" James asked hesitantly.

"Yeah. I'll let you go second." Art snickered loudly, as if he had cracked a really funny joke.

Christina was panting loudly, hyperventilating. Her entire body shook. She turned her eyes from the infested pond below back to Art.

"Your friend Terri had quite a time of it down there this morning," Art told Christina. "You should have heard all the splashing."

He removed a pocket knife from his trousers and pulled open the blade. "Hold still," he instructed them both. "I'm going to cut your hands free. Give you a fighting chance. We'll see if you can swim for it."

He sliced the cord off Christina's wrists. Then he worked on James's.

"I just don't believe Jack," Art muttered. James shook his freed hands, trying to get some feeling back in them. "He keeps those guys down there so *hungry!*"

He replaced the knife in his pants pocket and raised the gun to Christina's back.

"Do you want to jump or be pushed?" he asked her, his expression instantly turning hard, his voice low and menacing.

"Please!" Christina cried, shaking all over.

"Jump or be pushed?" Art repeated.

Christina grabbed her hair and tugged at it frantically. "Oh, please."

"Okay. I'll decide," Art said.

He drew back both arms and then with a burst of power, gave Christina a hard push.

Chapter 27

As Art pushed her, Christina dropped to her knees.

"No!" Art cried out in horror.

But he couldn't stop himself.

His motion carried him forward, over the edge of the precipice.

He reached out with both hands as if trying to grab onto something.

But he grabbed only air.

James saw the startled look on Art's face, the surprise quickly replaced by fear. And then he watched as Art plummeted down, his arms flailing frantically. Helplessly.

Art hit the green-brown water with a loud *smack*.

A perfect belly flop, James thought grimly.

Smack.

Waves tossed up, then crashed down with a splash.

Art disappeared under the rolling, murky waters.

The still pond suddenly came alive.

Peering down at the tossing water, James saw small shadows appear just under the surface, dozens and dozens of dark ripples darting rapidly, all in the same direction.

Art reappeared inside a rippling circle. First, his head emerged, and then both arms, reaching, reaching up like someone trying to climb a ladder.

Countless darting shadows closed in on him from all sides.

Art's arms thrashed the water.

He opened his mouth in a silent scream just before his head dipped again below the surface.

The waters tossed wildly. Art thrashed and kicked, stirring the water, sending out wave after wave.

His head resurfaced. His body jerked and twisted, as if he were fighting an invisible enemy.

His legs kicked frantically. His hands slapped the surface.

And then James, staring down in horror and fascination, saw a deep cut on Art's back. And then another. And cuts on Art's arms. And a deep gash on his side.

Struggling desperately, bobbing and twisting in the choppy water, his arms churning in place, Art went flailing under the surface again.

It's like he's being sucked down, James thought.

And then he saw that the water was red now. Red as blood.

Red as Art's blood.

Swirls of red in the tossing froth.

Puddles of red. Circles of red widening over the surface.

Art resurfaced one more time.

One arm reached for the sky.

The other hung lifelessly in the red water.

Chunks of flesh had been eaten away. Art floated in a circle of dark blood. His head bobbed on the surface like a wooden buoy, cut and bleeding.

James saw the deep gash at Art's throat. Saw bone exposed at Art's shoulder. Saw the fleshless legs float to the top, no longer kicking.

And with Art no longer kicking and thrashing, no longer moving, no longer making a sound, James heard the clicking of teeth, the chomping of flesh, the steady chewing and tearing.

And then the dark circle of blood blanketed what was left of Art's body. The body sank from view.

The dark shadows continued to snap and chew.

James finally forced himself to turn away as Art's body sank below the waters for good.

The terrifying sound of the clicking teeth, the tearing flesh still in his ears, James bent down to Christina. She hadn't changed her position. She was still on her knees, her hands covering her face, her entire body trembling.

"He's dead," James reported softly, kneeling beside her.

She didn't react.

At first, James thought she was crying. But as Christina lowered her hands from her face, he saw that her face was dry, her eyes clear.

"Art's dead," James repeated. "The piranhas — they chewed him to pieces."

"How horrible," she whispered, staring at the ground.

"Can you get up?" James asked. He reached for her arm to help her to her feet. "We have to get out of here."

She raised her eyes to his, her expression bewildered. "Out of here?"

James nodded. "We have to go to the police or something. We have to tell them about Art. And Terri."

Christina continued to stare at him. She made no attempt to stand up. Then, shaking her head, she lowered her eyes to the ground.

"Christina — are you okay? Can you get up?" He stood up and again reached to help her. "Let's get out of here," he urged. He shuddered, thinking about the clicking teeth, the widening pool of blood. "I want to get as far away from here as I can."

"But you can't," she said quietly.

"Huh?"

"You *can't* leave," Christina said. She leaned forward and picked up something from the ground at the edge of the precipice.

Art's pistol.

She pointed it up at James.

Her hand was steady now, he noticed. She was no longer trembling.

"You can't leave, James," she said. "You have to take a swim, too."

Chapter 28

"Hey, wait!" James took a step back. Then another.

Christina climbed quickly to her feet. "Don't run away," she said quietly. She aimed the pistol at his chest.

"But, why?" he cried.

"Stupid question," she said, sneering. "You're stupid, James."

"Yeah, you're right," he agreed. He raised his hands into a T, signaling for time out. "Okay, okay. Let's forget the police. Forget Art. Forget Art's father. Everything. Let's just get out of here."

Christina shook her head. "Not *us*. Just me," she said coldly.

"We'll go our separate ways," James said, staring over her shoulder to the shadowy, tangled woods. "We'll just split. We'll never see each other again. We'll never talk about any of it. To anyone. Okay?"

She lowered the pistol to her waist. "Not okay," she said flatly, her face expressionless, peering at him coldly through tangles of curls.

"Christina — I promise. My lips are sealed." He

moved his finger across his mouth as if zipping it up. "Be reasonable."

"I am being reasonable," she replied. "You're the only other person who knows what happened this week, James. The only one who knows about the old man, the stolen car, about Art."

"Yes, I know. But — " James continued to stare over Christina's shoulder.

"So if you take a swim with the piranhas, that leaves only one person who knows," Christina said. "Me. And I trust me. I'm the only one I trust. I'm walking away from here, James. I'm walking away, and you're not."

She raised the pistol and motioned with it toward the precipice edge. "Dive in, James. Now."

"Christina — wait!"

"Dive in. Don't make me shoot you first."

"Christina!"

"Maybe you'll get lucky. Maybe you'll drown before the piranhas attack."

"And what if I won't dive?" He took a step toward her.

She steadied the pistol, aiming it at his chest. "I'm going to count to three. If you don't dive, I'll shoot. Then I'll push you over the side."

"Wow, you're cold," James said, shaking his head. "You're cold."

"I have to be," she said softly. "Stop stalling."

"I don't believe you'll pull the trigger," he said.

"Don't test me," she snapped back. "You'll lose." She motioned with the pistol toward the precipice. "One."

"Come on, Christina — you and I . . ."

She uttered a scornful laugh. "You really are stupid, James. Two."

"You're not going to shoot me," he insisted.

"Yes. I guess I am," she replied. "And then I'm *out* of here."

"*No, you're not!*" declared a voice from behind Christina.

Chapter 29

Christina wheeled around at the sound of the voice.

A ragged, blood-soaked figure staggered toward them.

Christina recognized her immediately. "Terri!" she screamed.

Dragging one leg, Terri lumbered closer. James had been watching her over Christina's shoulder, waiting for her to make her move. Now he saw that she was carrying a large white rock.

"Terri!" Christina repeated. "But — how — ?"

Terri's dark hair hung down in damp tangles around her face. Her arms and legs were lined with jagged, deep cuts. Her denim cutoffs and midriff top were torn and bloodstained. One side of her face was caked with brown, dried blood.

Ignoring Christina's cries of surprise, Terri staggered forward.

"Terri — no! What are you *doing*?" Christina cried, taking a step back toward the edge of the precipice.

Glaring at Christina, her eyes wild with fury,

panting loudly with each step, Terri raised the rock.

Christina took another step back. "Terri — don't!"

Groaning from the effort, Terri lifted the rock above her head, preparing to heave it at Christina.

If Christina takes one more step back, she'll fall over the edge, James thought, watching the scene in silent horror. She's so frightened and so surprised to see Terri alive, she's forgotten about the pistol in her hand.

I'm saved, James thought gratefully.

One more step back, Christina. One more step. And Terri and I will be *outta* here!

With a loud cry, Terri pulled back the stone and started to throw it.

One more step, Christina, James silently urged. One more step back.

But to James's surprise, Christina lunged forward instead. Letting the pistol fall, she grabbed Terri's upraised arms — and swung her over the cliff edge.

James gasped as he heard the sickening splash.

Terri's gone this time, he thought.

Christina had already picked up the pistol. "No one left to save you now," she said, breathing hard. She pointed the pistol to the edge. "Go ahead. Jump."

Chapter 30

"Jump!" Christina shouted.

James felt the anger rise up from his chest, felt the red anger push away his fear.

He took a step toward the precipice edge. Then another.

"Jump!" Christina screamed.

Then James kicked as hard as he could.

Christina couldn't move in time. James's shoe struck her wrist. She howled in pain and surprise. The gun flew up — and over the precipice.

They both heard it splash down below.

And then they were wrestling, struggling, at the edge, groaning and crying out as they stood grappling, pushing, tearing at each other, trying to shove the other over the side.

"No! No! No!" Christina shrieked as James wrapped his powerful arms around her waist, tried to push her off-balance.

Over, over *over*! The word repeated silently in his mind as he tried to wrestle her down.

"Ohh!" He uttered a pained wail as she brought

her knee up hard to his stomach. He gasped for air. His muscles collapsed. He dropped to his knees.

I'm dead, he thought.

I'm dead now.

She stood over him, ready to finish him off.

He lowered his head — and saw a hand raise up behind Christina. A hand from below. A hand reaching up from the cliff.

The hand grabbed Christina's ankles.

And pulled.

Christina's mouth opened into a wide O of horror as she lost her balance and was pulled over the side of the precipice.

James heard the splash. And then the frantic thrashing. The cries for help. The churning water. The click of piranha teeth. The screams, more and more pained and pitiful.

And then silence.

Leaning over the edge, he saw Terri clinging to a tree root sticking out from the cliff. He reached down and grabbed one hand. Then the other. And then he pulled with all of his remaining strength.

"Help me," Terri moaned, crawling to safety on the ground, collapsing onto her stomach. She raised a bleeding arm up to James. "Please."

"I heard you fall," James uttered, struggling to clear his head. "I heard the splash."

"That was the rock," she told him. "The rock fell. I grabbed the side. There was a tree root. I grabbed it and — ohh. Please, help me."

"There's got to be a hospital around here," James said. "We'll take Art's car."

With the sound of Christina's final anguished cries still wailing like a police siren in his ears, he bent to lift Terri to her feet.

The two policemen nodded to James as they walked out of Terri's room. They had already questioned James for hours. He had patiently told them everything he knew, everything that had happened to him since being picked up by Terri and Christina. Now they were finally leaving Terri's hospital room after questioning her.

James watched them head down the long hospital corridor, glancing at their notepads as they talked. When they turned a corner and were out of sight, he stepped into Terri's room.

She smiled at him. She had stitches along one cheek. She had the bedsheet pulled up nearly to her chin.

"I just came to say good-bye," James said, standing awkwardly in the doorway.

She motioned for him to pull up the folding chair against the wall.

"No. I've really got to be going," he told her.

Why did hospitals make him sweat so much?

"Thanks for getting me here," Terri said shyly. "I guess you're sorry you ever hitched a ride with Christina and me."

"Yeah. I am," he replied honestly, then smiled.

"I tried to get Christina to go to the police," Terri said, frowning. "I really tried. After she hit the old man, I didn't want to go on. I wanted to turn ourselves in. That's what we were arguing about all the time."

James scratched his head. He leaned against the wall. "I'm so stupid," he said, grinning. "I thought you two were fighting about *me!*"

Terri laughed. "Ouch! Don't make me laugh!" she cried. "How can you be so conceited?"

James shrugged.

"I didn't want to stop and pick you up," Terri said. "I knew Christina and I were in real big trouble. I didn't see the point of involving you in it. But Christina thought it would be a hoot. She said she could use a distraction."

"I was a distraction?" James cried.

"We fought about it, but I lost. That's why I was so cold to you in the beginning. I was trying to warn you that you had gotten yourself into trouble."

"What about the night at the motel? You came to my room and — "

"Christina made me do that," Terri explained. "We were fighting in the motel about whether or not to dump the car. Finally, she won. She wanted you out of the way so she could go hide the car. And then, after we got back from the woods, she . . ."

Her voice broke. Her eyes filled with tears.

"She asked me if I wanted to see where she hid the car. I said no, I didn't care. But she insisted I come with her. She led me into a different area of woods. Very swampy. Then she said she couldn't take the chance of me wimping out. I was too big a risk, she said. She hit me. With a heavy tree branch. Hit me again and again. I went down. I pretended to be dead. She thought she killed me. So she went back to the motel."

"So cold," James said softly. "So cold." He shifted his weight, crossing his arms over his chest. "Then what happened?"

"I was pretty badly beat up," Terri told him, smoothing the bedcovers with one hand. "I looked up. I guess I was real groggy. And there was a man staring down at me. It was Art."

"He took you to the cabin?"

"Early this morning. He pushed me into the piranha pond. It — it was a nightmare. But I got out. He didn't know what a good swimmer I am. Even *I* didn't know I was that good. Somehow I managed to get out. Art didn't even wait to see if I was dead. He was in such a hurry to drive back and pick you up."

"And then you waited in the swamp?" James asked.

"I think I passed out for a while. I must have been in shock. Then I heard voices. I saw you and Christina. I saw what was happening." She swallowed hard and closed her eyes. "You know the rest."

"You saved my life," James said.

"You saved mine, too," Terri replied, opening her eyes and smiling at him. "I guess that makes us almost even." She glanced down at his canvas bag. "Where are you going now? Further north?"

"No." He shook his head. "Back to Key West."

"Back home?"

"Yeah. There's a girl there. Her name's Melissa.

I hurt her really badly. I want to go back and — "

"You hurt her?"

"Well . . . I broke up with her. It hurt her really bad. She — "

"You really *are* a conceited pig!" Terri laughed.

Her remark caught James by surprise. He stopped short, a thoughtful expression freezing his face.

Terri was probably right. Melissa was hurt, but not as badly as he wanted to think.

He laughed, too. "Guess I'll be going. You'll be okay?" He picked up his bag.

"Yeah. My parents are on their way," Terri said.

He started out the door.

"How are you getting home?" Terri called after him.

"Hitching," he told her.

"Good luck!" she said.

About the Author

R.L. STINE is the author of more than two dozen thrillers for young readers. Recent titles include *Beach House* and *Hit and Run*. He is also the author of two series — *Fear Street* and *Goosebumps*.

In addition to his publishing work, he is head writer of the TV show *Eureeka's Castle*, seen on Nickelodeon.

He lives in New York City with his wife, Jane, and their twelve-year-old son, Matt.

THRILLERS

point ®

Other books you will enjoy,
about real kids like you!

☐ MZ43469-1	**Arly** Robert Newton Peck	$2.95
☐ MZ40515-2	**City Light** Harry Mazer	$2.75
☐ MZ44494-8	**Enter Three Witches** Kate Gilmore	$2.95
☐ MZ40943-3	**Fallen Angels** Walter Dean Myers	$3.50
☐ MZ40847-X	**First a Dream** Maureen Daly	$3.25
☐ MZ43020-3	**Handsome as Anything** Merrill Joan Gerber	$2.95
☐ MZ43999-5	**Just a Summer Romance** Ann M. Martin	$2.75
☐ MZ44629-0	**Last Dance** Caroline B. Cooney	$2.95
☐ MZ44628-2	**Life Without Friends** Ellen Emerson White	$2.95
☐ MZ42769-5	**Losing Joe's Place** Gordon Korman	$2.95
☐ MZ43664-3	**A Pack of Lies** Geraldine McCaughrean	$2.95
☐ MZ43419-5	**Pocket Change** Kathryn Jensen	$2.95
☐ MZ43821-2	**A Royal Pain** Ellen Conford	$2.95
☐ MZ44429-8	**A Semester in the Life of a Garbage Bag** Gordon Korman	$2.95
☐ MZ43867-0	**Son of Interflux** Gordon Korman	$2.95
☐ MZ43971-5	**The Stepfather Game** Norah McClintock	$2.95
☐ MZ41513-1	**The Tricksters** Margaret Mahy	$2.95
☐ MZ43638-4	**Up Country** Alden R. Carter	$2.95

Watch for new titles coming soon!
Available wherever you buy books, or use this order form.

Scholastic Inc., P.O. Box 7502, 2931 E. McCarty Street, Jefferson City, MO 65102

Please send me the books I have checked above. I am enclosing $ _____
Please add $2.00 to cover shipping and handling. Send check or money order - no cash or C.O.D's please.

Name _____

Address _____

City _____ State/Zip _____

Please allow four to six weeks for delivery. Offer good in U.S.A. only. Sorry, mail orders are not available to residents of Canada. Prices subject to changes.

PNT891

point ®

THRILLERS

R.L. Stine
☐ MC44236-8 The Baby-sitter $3.50
☐ MC44332-1 The Baby-sitter II $3.50
☐ MC45386-6 Beach House $3.25
☐ MC43278-8 Beach Party $3.50
☐ MC43125-0 Blind Date $3.50
☐ MC43279-6 The Boyfriend $3.50
☐ MC44333-X The Girlfriend $3.50
☐ MC45385-8 Hit and Run $3.25
☐ MC46100-1 The Hitchhiker $3.50
☐ MC43280-X The Snowman $3.50
☐ MC43139-0 Twisted $3.50

Caroline B. Cooney
☐ MC44316-X The Cheerleader $3.25
☐ MC41641-3 The Fire $3.25
☐ MC43806-9 The Fog $3.25
☐ MC45681-4 Freeze Tag $3.25
☐ MC45402-1 The Perfume $3.25
☐ MC44884-6 The Return of the
        Vampire $2.95
☐ MC41640-5 The Snow $3.25
☐ MC45682-2 The Vampire's
        Promise $3.50

Diane Hoh
☐ MC44330-5 The Accident $3.25
☐ MC45401-3 The Fever $3.25
☐ MC43050-5 Funhouse $3.25
☐ MC44904-4 The Invitation $3.50
☐ MC45640-7 The Train (9/92) $3.25

Sinclair Smith
☐ MC45063-8 The Waitress $2.95

Christopher Pike
☐ MC43014-9 Slumber Party $3.50
☐ MC44256-2 Weekend $3.50

A. Bates
☐ MC45829-9 The Dead
        Game $3.25
☐ MC43291-5 Final Exam $3.25
☐ MC44582-0 Mother's Helper $3.50
☐ MC44238-4 Party Line $3.25

D.E. Athkins
☐ MC45246-0 Mirror, Mirror $3.25
☐ MC45349-1 The Ripper $3.25
☐ MC44941-9 Sister Dearest $2.95

Carol Ellis
☐ MC44768-8 My Secret
        Admirer $3.25
☐ MC46044-7 The Stepdaughter $3.25
☐ MC44916-8 The Window $2.95

Richie Tankersley Cusick
☐ MC43115-3 April Fools $3.25
☐ MC43203-6 The Lifeguard $3.25
☐ MC43114-5 Teacher's Pet $3.25
☐ MC44235-X Trick or Treat $3.25

Lael Littke
☐ MC44237-6 Prom Dress $3.25

Edited by T. Pines
☐ MC45256-8 Thirteen $3.50

Available wherever you buy books, or use this order form.